Maverick
vs. Maverick

—

Shirley Jump

P9-BYI-361

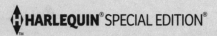

HARLEQUIN® SPECIAL EDITION®

Special thanks and acknowledgment are given to Shirley Jump for her contribution to the Montana Mavericks: The Baby Bonanza continuity.

Recycling programs
for this product may
not exist in your area.

ISBN-13: 978-0-373-65986-9

Maverick vs. Maverick

Copyright © 2016 by Harlequin Books S.A.

Printed in U.S.A.

www.Harlequin.com

New York Times and *USA TODAY* bestselling author **Shirley Jump** spends her days writing romance so she can avoid the towering stack of dirty dishes, eat copious amounts of chocolate and reward herself with trips to the mall. Visit her website at shirleyjump.com for author news and a booklist, and follow her at Facebook.com/shirleyjump.author for giveaways and deep discussions about important things like chocolate and shoes.

To the family I was born into and the family of friends I have found along the way—thank you for always having my back and for the steady supply of belly-deep laughter and warm, sweet memories.

Chapter One

Walker Jones's mother would tell anyone who would listen that her oldest son came into this world ready to argue. He was a carbon copy of his father that way, she'd say, another man ready to debate everything from the color of the sky to the temperature of the room.

So it was no surprise he'd grown up to fill his father's shoes in the boardroom, too.

The elder, Walker Jones II, was a formidable opponent in any corporate environment, though his advanced age had warranted a decline in the number of hours he worked. Walker III had stepped in, doubling the company in size and reach. That desire to take over the world had led him to do the one thing he thought he'd never do again—journey back to small-town America to defend the family business interests.

Walker had grown up in Oklahoma, but as far as he could tell, Rust Creek Falls and Kalispell, Montana, where the courthouse was located, were just copycats of the kind of tiny spit of a town that Walker tried to avoid. Lord knew what his brother Hudson saw in the place, because to Walker, it was just one more Norman Rockwell painting to escape as soon as humanly possible. He'd spent as little time as possible here a few months earlier when he'd opened his first Just Us Kids Day Care center. Basically just enough time to unlock the door and hand Hudson the keys. The day care center was a tiny part of the much larger operation of Jones Holdings, Inc., a blip on the corporate radar.

Walker had no intention of staying any longer this time around, either. Just long enough to deal with a pesky lawsuit and a persistent lawyer named Lindsay Dalton. The attorney worked in her father's office. Probably one of those kids handed a job regardless of their competency level, Walker scoffed. He figured he'd make quick work of the whole thing and get back to his corporate offices in Tulsa ASAP.

Walker strode into Judge Sheldon Andrews's courtroom on a Friday morning, figuring he could be out of town by sunset. The lawsuit was frivolous, the charges unfounded, and Walker had no doubt he could get it thrown out before the arguments got started.

Walker shrugged out of his cashmere overcoat, placed it neatly on the back of his chair, then settled himself behind the wide oak defendant's table. He laid a legal pad before him, a file folder on his left, and a row of pens to the right. Props, really, part of sending a message to the plaintiff that Walker was ready for a fight. Perception, Walker had learned, was half the battle. His lawyer, Marty Peyton, who had been around the courtroom longer than Walker had been alive, came in and took the seat beside him.

"This summary judgment should be a slam dunk," Walker said to Marty. "These claims are totally groundless."

"I don't know if I'd call it a slam dunk," Marty whispered back. He pushed his glasses up his nose and ran a hand through his short white hair. "If Lindsay Dalton is anything like her father, she's a great lawyer."

Walker waved that off. He'd gone up against more formidable opponents than some small-town lawyer.

"And for another, this is about sick kids," Marty went on. "You already have the court of public opinion against you."

"Sick *kid*, singular," Walker corrected. "She's only representing one family. And kids get sick at day care centers all the time. Kids are walking germ factories."

Marty pursed his lips and sat back in his seat. "Whatever you say. I hope you're right. You don't need this kind of publicity, especially since you're planning to open five more locations this year."

The new locations would bring the day care division up to twenty-two locations, throughout Montana and Oklahoma. A nice dent in the western market. "It'll be fine. We'll dispense with this lawyer and her ridiculous suit before you can say hello and goodbye." Walker straightened the pens again, then turned when the courtroom door opened and in walked his opponent.

Lindsay Dalton was not what he'd been expecting. Not even close.

Given the terse tone of her letters and voice mails, he'd expected some librarian type. All buttoned up and severe, with glasses and a shapeless, dingy brown jacket. Instead, he got a five-foot-five cover model in a pale gray suit and a pink silk shirt with the top two buttons unfastened. Not to mention heels and incredible legs.

She was, in a word, fascinating.

Lindsay Dalton had long brown hair in a tidy ponytail that skimmed the back of her suit and bangs that dusted across her forehead. Her big blue eyes were accented by a touch of makeup. Just enough to draw his gaze to her face, then focus it on her lips.

She smiled at her clients just then—a young couple who looked like they'd donned their Sunday best—and the smile was what hit Walker the hardest. It was dazzling. Powerful.

Holy hell.

He turned to Marty. "*That's* Lindsay Dalton?"

Marty shrugged. "I guess so. Pretty girl."

"Good looks doesn't make her a good lawyer," Walker said. She might be a bit distracting, but that didn't mean his lawyer couldn't argue against her and get this case thrown out.

She walked to the front of the courtroom, not sparing a glance at either Walker or Marty, then took her seat on the plaintiff's side, with her clients on her right. An older woman, probably a grandma, sat in the gallery with the couple's baby on her lap. Lindsay turned and gave the baby a big grin. The child cooed. Lindsay covered her eyes for a second, opened her hands like a book, and whispered "peekaboo." The baby giggled and Lindsay repeated the action twice more, before turning back to the front of the courtroom.

It was a sweet, tender moment, but Walker knew full well that Lindsay Dalton had arranged to have the baby here, not for silly games, but to garner some sympathy points.

The door behind the judge's bench opened and Judge Andrews stepped out. Short, bespectacled and a little on the pudgy side, Judge Andrews resembled a heavy Bob Newhart. The bailiff called, "All rise," and everyone stood while Andrews gave the courtroom a nod, then took his place on the bench.

"You may be seated," he said. Then the bailiff called the court to order, and they got under way.

This was the part Walker liked the best, whether it was in courtroom or in the boardroom. That eager anticipation in his gut just before everything started. Like two armies squaring off across the battlefield, with the tension so high it charged the air.

"We're here on your motion for a summary judgment regarding the lawsuit brought by the plaintiffs, represented by Ms. Dalton, correct?" Judge Andrews asked Walker's attorney.

"Yes, Your Honor."

The judge waved at the podium. "Then, Mr. Peyton, you may proceed."

"Thank you, Your Honor." Marty got to his feet and laid his notes before him on the table. "This lawsuit, brought against Mr. Jones's day care center, is a waste of everyone's time. There is simply no legal or factual basis for the suit. Ms. Dalton is trying to prove that her client's child caught a cold at the center, but there is no evidence whatsoever to support that claim. Germs are a fact of life, Your Honor. They're on any surface we touch, and no one can prove that the Marshalls' child contracted a common cold because of her time in day care. Why, for all we know, one of the Marshalls could have brought the germs into their own house. All it takes is one sneeze from a stranger or contact with a germ-infested surface in a public place. Surely Ms. Dalton can't blame Mr. Jones's day care center for the world's inability to reach for a Kleenex at the right time."

That was a line Walker had given Marty in their meeting last week. It seemed to amuse the judge. A smile ghosted on his face then disappeared.

"Your Honor," Marty continued, "there are no cases holding that a day care center is legally responsible when a child who spends part of her day there comes down with a cold. Frankly, it's a frivolous claim, and we're asking that the court enter summary judgment in the defendant's favor, dismissing this case."

Judge Andrews nodded at Marty, then turned to Lindsay Dalton. "Ms. Dalton?"

Lindsay got to her feet and smoothed a hand down the front of her jacket. She took a moment to draw in a breath, as if centering herself.

She was nervous. *Good*, Walker thought. He had this thing won already.

"Your Honor, Mr. Peyton is greatly minimizing the situation at hand. This was not a common cold, not by any means. We intend to prove that Mr. Jones's day care center, Just Us Kids, has been grossly negligent in cleanliness, resulting in a severe respiratory syncytial virus infection for Georgina Marshall, the then three-month-old child of Peter and Heather Marshall. The Marshalls entrusted Mr. Jones's day care center with the care of their precious child, only to end up sitting by her hospital bed, praying for her to overcome the bronchitis that developed as a result of her exposure to RSV."

Walker fought the urge to roll his eyes. *Precious child? Praying?*

"Your Honor, RSV is a respiratory infection," Marty said, standing up again. "It's marked by a cough and runny nose. Just like the common cold."

"Georgina stopped eating," Lindsay countered. "She lost two pounds, which for a baby of her size is a dramatic weight loss. The hospital she was in didn't see this as a common cold. They saw it as a life-threatening illness. A life-threatening illness caused by Mr. Jones's negligence." With those words she turned and glared directly at Walker.

As if he was the one neglecting to mop the floors and wipe down the toys every night. Walker had barely stepped inside the day care center in Rust Creek Falls. He'd left his brother Hudson to oversee the business and hired a highly experienced and competent manager to help run the place. He had no doubt that Just Us Kids was running as smoothly as a Swiss watch.

He was busy enough maintaining the corporate interests. He had oil wells in Texas and overseas, the financial division expanding in the northeast, and then these day care centers, all started in small towns because his research had shown they were the most in need of child care resources.

Ms. Dalton rushed on. "Your Honor, I invite you to read the medical charts, which we filed with the court in opposition to the defendant's motion for summary judgment. Those alone will prove how close the Marshalls came to losing their only child."

Marty got to his feet. "Your Honor, does the Marshalls' counsel really need to use words like 'precious'? All children are precious, and no disrespect to the Marshalls, but their child is no more precious than anyone else's. Can we stick to facts, without the flowery language?"

"The facts are clear, Your Honor," Lindsay said. "The Marshalls' baby contracted RSV as a direct result of staying in Mr. Jones's day care. As did many other children—"

"This case is only about the Marshalls," Walker interjected. "It's one family, not a class action."

She wheeled on him and shot him a glare. "They merely want justice for the pain and suffering their daughter endured."

Code for *give us a big settlement so we never have to work again.* Walker bit back a sigh. He was tired of people who used the justice system to make a quick buck.

"The child is healthy now," Walker said to the judge, despite Marty waving a hand to silence him. "This was a short-lived illness, and again, not traceable to any one contaminant. To blame my day care center is casting a pretty specific net in a very large river."

The judge gave him a stern look. "Mr. Walker, I'll thank you to leave the argument to your lawyer. You're not here testifying today."

"I apologize for my client's outburst, Your Honor," Marty said smoothly. "It's just that this is so clearly a frivolous claim. Which is why we are moving to have this case dismissed before it wastes any more of the court's time."

Judge Andrews nodded again, and both lawyers sat to wait for him to announce his ruling. He flipped through the papers before him, taking a few minutes to scan the documents.

Walker sat at his table, maintaining a calm demeanor, as if this whole thing was a walk in the park. In all honesty, though, if he lost this case, it could severely impact his whole company and the future of the entire Just Us Kids Day Care chain. He refused to let some small-town lawyer derail his future expansion plans. Jones Holdings, Inc. was solid enough to withstand this tiny dent, but he wasn't so sure the day care centers could rise above the ensuing bad publicity if the case wasn't dismissed. Walker was in this business to make a profit, not to see it wiped away by some overeager small-town lawyer.

Lindsay Dalton had her legs crossed, right over left, and her right foot swung back and forth in a tight, nervous arc under the table. She whispered something to Heather Marshall, who nodded then covered Lindsay's hand with her own and gave it a squeeze. Heather Marshall's eyes watered—whether for real or for effect, Walker couldn't tell. He'd seen enough people fake emotions in business that a few tears no longer swayed him.

Judge Andrews cleared his throat and looked up from his paperwork. "It's the opinion of this court that there is sufficient evidence to proceed to trial on this case." He put up a hand to ward off Marty's objections, then lowered his glasses and looked at Walker's attorney. "Mr. Peyton, you and your client may think this suit is frivolous, but the evidence Ms. Dalton has offered demonstrates that there are genuine issues of material fact. Now, let's talk about a date for the trial. I realize we had set a date for four weeks from today, but that date will no longer work for me. As part of the joys of getting old, I have to have a knee replaced, and am not sure how long I will be out."

Great. That would just make this thing drag on longer and longer. Walker didn't need the prolonged negative publicity.

"But thanks to a big case settling just this morning, my schedule for next week has an unexpected hole in it and I can hear your arguments on Tuesday morning, after the Columbus Day holiday."

Lindsay Dalton shot to her feet. "Objection, Your Honor. I need more time to adequately prepare—"

"From what I have seen, you are prepared, Ms. Dalton. Tuesday is the date, unless you and your clients want to prolong this case indefinitely." The Marshalls shook their head, and Lindsay nodded acceptance. "Good. I will see you all back here Tuesday at 9:00 a.m. Court dismissed." He banged the gavel, then got to his feet.

Everyone rose and waited until the judge had exited the courtroom, before the lawyers turned to gather their papers. Walker leaned toward Marty. "Temporary setback."

Marty gave him a dubious look. "I told you, she may be new, but we have our work cut out for us."

"Piece of cake," Walker said. "Don't worry."

The Marshalls walked by him, holding hands and

giving Lindsay wavering smiles. The Marshalls didn't look like frivolous lawsuit people, and Lindsay Dalton didn't look like a crappy small-town lawyer hired by her daddy. She looked like one of those ridiculously nice, highly principled people who only wanted to do the right thing to brighten their corner of the world. But Walker knew better. She wasn't here to play nice and he wasn't about to let her win, even if this schedule change threw a giant monkey wrench into his plans.

One that meant there was a very, very strong possibility that Walker Jones was going to be in Rust Creek Falls a lot longer than he had thought.

The mirrored wall behind the bar at Ace in the Hole was good for reflecting a lot more than the alcohol bottles lined up on the shelf, Lindsay Dalton realized. It also showed her own frustrated features. Even now, hours after she'd left the courtroom and her first battle against Walker Jones, Lindsay was feeling anxious, stressed. Yes, she'd won today—a small victory—but that first argument was just the beginning. And her opponent was not who she had expected.

She'd done her research on Walker Jones, or at least she thought she had. An older gentleman—heck, almost at retirement age—who she had thought would be an easy opponent. She clearly hadn't researched enough, because the man sitting in the courtroom today wasn't old and frail. He was young and handsome and...

Formidable.

Yes, that was the right word to describe Walker Jones III. Formidable. He had an easy confidence about him, an attitude that said he knew what he was doing and he wasn't used to losing.

And she was a brand-new lawyer from a small town working for her father's firm. She had convictions and confidence, but that might not be enough to win against experience and attitude. And a big-time lawyer hired from out of town.

"Looks like you had the kind of day that needs this." Lani slid a glass of chardonnay over to Lindsay. Her sister worked at the bar from time to time, even after getting engaged to Russ Campbell, the hunky cop she'd fallen in love a little over a year ago. Lani still had a glow about her, shining nearly as brightly as the engagement ring on her finger.

"Thanks," Lindsay said. "I didn't expect to see you at the Ace tonight."

Lani shrugged. "The bar was short staffed. Annie had a date and asked me to fill in."

Annie Kellerman, the regular bartender. The Ace in the Hole was pretty much the main watering hole in Rust Creek Falls. With hitching posts outside and neon beer signs inside, it was the kind of place where folks could let down their hair, have a few beers with friends and maybe take a fast twirl in front of the jukebox. Since it was early yet on a Friday night, the Ace wasn't too busy—one couple snuggling in a booth, four guys debating last week's football game at a table in the center of the room and a couple of regulars sitting at the end of the bar, nursing longneck beers and watching whatever sport was playing on the overhead TV.

"So, how'd it go in court today?" Lani asked. She had her long brown hair back in a clip and was wearing a tank top with the logo for the bar—an ace of hearts—across the front.

"I won." Lindsay grinned. "Okay, so it was only winning the argument that I brought a valid case to court, but it sure made me feel good."

"Given all the times you've argued with me, little sister, I have no doubt you're going to make a great lawyer." Lani swiped at a water ring on the bar, then leaned back against the shelf behind her. "I talked to Dad earlier and he's proud as a peacock. I'm surprised he didn't take out a billboard announcing the judge's decision."

Lindsay laughed. Their father, Ben, had been ready to burst at the seams from the day she told him she wanted to follow in his footsteps. "It's a very small decision. The big case is yet to come. I have a few days until opening arguments." She let out a breath. "I'm nervous as hell."

"Why? You're a great lawyer."

"For one, I only passed the bar a few months ago. My experience is mainly in cases like whether George Lambert's oak tree is encroaching on Lee Reynolds's potato patch." Because she was so new to her father's firm, he generally shuffled the easy stuff over to Lindsay's desk, as a way for her to get her feet wet. She'd argued ownership of a Pomeranian, defended a driver who took a left on red and settled the aforementioned potato patch/oak tree dispute.

"Which was a win for you," Lani pointed out.

Lindsay scoffed. She'd become a lawyer because she wanted to make a difference in the town she loved. So far, she'd only made a difference for a Pomeranian and a garden. She was worried she wasn't up to the challenge of battling for the Marshalls. But when they had come to her, worried and teary, she couldn't say no. She might be inexperienced, but she had a fire for what was right burning in her belly. She couldn't stand to see anyone get hurt because the Just Us Kids Day Care was negligent. "Score one for the potatoes. Seriously, though, the opposing counsel in this case is…good. Smart. And the owner of the day care center is just as smart. Plus, he's handsome."

Had she just said that out loud? Good Lord.

Lani arched a brow. "Handsome?"

"I meant attractive." Oh, God, that wasn't any better. Lindsay scrambled to come up with a way to describe Walker Jones that didn't make it sound like she personally found him sexy. Because she didn't. At all. Even if he had filled out his navy pin-striped suit like a model for Brooks Brothers. He was the enemy, and even handsome men could be irresponsible business owners. "In a distracting kind of way. He might… sway the judge."

Lani chuckled. "Judge Andrews? Isn't he like, a hundred?"

"Well, yeah, but…" Lindsay drained her wine and held her glass out to her sister. "Can I get a refill?"

"Is that your way of changing the subject?" Lani took the glass and topped it off.

"Yes. No." She paused. She'd been disconcerted by meeting Walker Jones, and Lindsay didn't get disconcerted easily. "Maybe."

"Well, unfortunately, I don't think you're going to be able to do that," Lani said as she slid the glass back to her sister.

"Come on, don't tell me you're going to ask me a

million questions about this guy. Frankly, I'd like to forget all about Walker Jones until I have to see him in court next week."

"I think it's going to be impossible for you to do that." Lani leaned across the bar and a tease lit her features. "Considering he just walked in. Or at least, a man who looks like a hot, sexy owner of a day care chain just walked in."

Lindsay spun on her stool and nearly choked on her sip of wine. Walker Jones III had indeed just walked into the Ace in the Hole, still wearing his overcoat and suit from court, and looking like a man ready to take over enemy territory. "What is he doing here?"

"Probably getting a drink like the rest of Rust Creek Falls," Lani said. "There's not a lot of options in this town."

"Why is he even still here? Why not stay in Kalispell, or better yet, why can't he go back to his coffin?"

"Coffin?"

"Only vampires are that handsome and ruthless."

Lani chuckled. She shifted to the center of the bar as Walker approached. "Welcome to the Ace in the Hole. What can I get you?"

"Woodford Reserve, on the rocks." He leaned one elbow on the bar, then shifted to his right.

"We don't have that," Lani said. "What we do have is a whole lot of beer."

Walker sighed. "Then your best craft beer."

"Coming right up."

Lindsay should have slipped off her stool and left before he noticed her, but she'd been so stunned at the sight of Walker in the Ace that she had stayed where she was, as if her butt had grown roots. Now she tried to take a casual sip of her wine, as if she didn't even see him.

Except her heart was racing, and all she could see out of the corner of her eye was him. Six feet tall—her favorite height in a man, but who was noticing that—with dirty blond hair and blue eyes, Walker Jones had a way of commanding the space where he stood.

She needed to remember that his irresponsible ownership of the day care center was what had made Georgina and lots of other children ill. What if that had been the Stockton triplets? Those motherless newborns who'd needed a whole chain of volunteers to help care for them? The RSV outbreak could have had much more dire consequences—something that Walker might be trying to overlook but that she refused to ignore.

"Counselor," he said with a little nod.

"Mr. Jones. Nice to see you again." The conventional greeting rolled off her tongue before she could recall it. Some kind of masochistic automatic response. It wasn't nice to see him again. Not one bit.

Lani smirked as she placed a beer in front of Walker. "Here you go. Want me to run a tab?"

"Thank you, and yes, please do. I think I'll stay a bit." He sent the last remark in Lindsay's direction.

She still had a nearly full glass of wine, but no way was she going to sit at the bar next to him. Lindsay fished in her pocket and handed her sister some bills. "Thanks, Lani. I'll see you around."

As Lindsay went to leave, Walker placed a hand on her arm. A momentary touch, nothing more, but it seemed to sear her skin. "Don't go because I'm here.

Surely we can coexist in a bar full of people." He looked around. "Or rather, a bar full of eleven people."

"Are you always this exact?"

"Are you always this hard to make friends with?"

She scowled. He was making it seem like this was all her fault. "We don't need to be friends. We're on opposing sides."

"In the courtroom. Outside of that, we can at least be civil, can't we?"

"Well, of course we can be civil." Damn it. Somehow he'd turned her whole argument around. Geesh. Maybe he should have been the lawyer.

"That's all I'm asking. So stay." He gestured toward her bar stool. "And pretend I don't exist."

"My pleasure."

That made him laugh. He had a nice laugh, dark and rich like a great cup of coffee in the morning. "You are not what I expected, Ms. Dalton."

"And you are not what I expected." She fiddled with the stem of her wineglass. "Frankly, I was expecting your father."

"Sorry to disappoint you." He grinned. "I'll try not to do that again."

She almost said, "Oh, I wasn't disappointed," but caught herself. Good Lord, what was it with this man? Was it his eyes? The way they held her gaze and made her, for just a moment, feel like the most important person in the room? Was it the way he'd touched her, his muscled hand seeming to leave an indelible impression? Or was it the way he spoke, in that deep, confident voice, that a part of her imagined him whispering to her in the dark?

He was the enemy. An evil, irresponsible man who

only cared about making a buck. Except nothing about his demeanor matched that description. Maybe he was one of those distracted, charming millionaires who didn't care where his money came from as long as it ended up in his bank account.

Still...he seemed nice. Friendly, even. How could that be the same man who ran a shoddy day care chain?

"And with that," Walker said, picking up his beer and giving her a little nod, "I think I shall leave you to your wine. Have a good evening, Ms. Dalton."

He crossed the room, and took a seat at one of the empty tables, draping his coat over a second chair. When a group of twenty-something girls came into the bar, ushering in the cool evening air and a whole bunch of laughter, Lindsay's view of Walker was blocked, but that didn't stop her traitorous mind from wondering what he'd meant by *I'll try not to do that again.*

Because she had a feeling Walker Jones was the kind of man who rarely left a woman disappointed. In any way.

Chapter Two

Walker didn't know why he'd stayed. Or why he lingered over his beer. Or why his gaze kept straying to Lindsay Dalton.

He told himself it was because he was so surprised to see her in ordinary clothes—jeans, cowboy boots and a blue button-down shirt with the cuffs rolled up to her forearms. The jeans hugged her thighs, outlined the curve of her butt and in general made Walker forget to breathe. He could imagine her wearing the dark brown cowboy boots and nothing else.

Okay, not productive. She was the opposing counsel in a lawsuit vital to the future of his day care centers. They may only be a small piece of the large pie that made up Jones Holdings, Inc., but that didn't matter. Walker was not a man who liked to lose. Ever.

The bar began to fill, and he noticed people glancing at him, either because he was a clear outsider or because word got around. There were friendly greetings for Lindsay but a definite chill in the air when it came to Walker. Clearly, the people of Rust Creek Falls were circling the wagons around one of their own.

Walker had debated flying back to his office in Tulsa after court ended today, but with the trial just a few days away, he'd decided to stay in town. It might be good to get to know the locals, get a feel for how things might sway in court and maybe make a few friends out of what might become a lynch mob if Lindsay Dalton had her way.

The best way to do all that? Alcohol, and lots of it.

Gaining the goodwill of the locals was merely part of Walker's overall plan. He would obliterate Lindsay Dalton's case, then leave the town thinking he was the hero, not the devil incarnate she'd made him out to be.

Walker strode back up to the bar, sending Lindsay a nod of greeting that she ignored. He put a hand on the smooth oak surface. "I want to buy a round," he said to the bartender.

The woman, slim and brunette, looked similar enough to Lindsay that Walker could believe they were related. Especially in a town this small. "Sure, for...who?" she said.

"Everyone." He grinned. "New in town. Figured it'd be a nice way to introduce myself."

"You mean try to convince people you're a nice guy?" Lindsay said from beside him.

"I am a nice guy. My grandmother and third-grade teacher said so." He grinned at her. "You just haven't given me a chance."

"And you think a free beer will change my mind?"

He leaned in closer to her, close enough to catch a whiff of her perfume, something dark and sensual, which surprised him. Oh, how he wished it was as simple as a beer to change her mind, because if they had met under different circumstances, he would have asked her out. She was fiery and gorgeous and confident, and he was intrigued. "If it would, I'd buy you a case."

"I'm not so easily bought, Mr. Jones."

"Then name your price, Ms. Dalton."

"An admission of guilt." Her blue eyes hardened. "And changes in the way you run your business."

Well, well. So the lawyer liked the fight as much as he did. There was nothing Walker liked better than a challenge. "A round for everyone in the bar, Miss…" He waved toward the bartender.

"Lani. Lani Dalton." The brunette leaned back against the counter and crossed her arms. "Sister to Lindsay."

That explained the defensive posture. Okay, so he had two enemies in Rust Creek Falls. He'd faced worse. Besides, he wasn't going to be here long. It wasn't going to matter what people said about him after he left—as long as he won the lawsuit and re-established the good reputation of Just Us Kids Day Care. All he needed to do while he was here was temporarily change public perception about himself. Winning the lawsuit would take care of the rest. So he put on a friendly smile and put out his hand. It wasn't making deals over drinks at a penthouse restaurant, but it would accomplish the same thing. And at a much cheaper price.

"Nice to meet you, Lani." They shook. "I'm Walker Jones, owner of Just Us Kids."

"Your day care has quite the tarnished reputation," Lani said. "Folks here have a pretty negative opinion after all those kids got sick."

Walker maintained his friendly smile. "An unfortunate event, to be sure. I'm hoping people will see that I'm a responsible owner, here to make things right."

Beside him on the stool, Lindsay snorted. He ignored the sound of derision.

The bar had begun to fill since he got here, and the people standing in the Ace in the Hole were making no secret of eavesdropping on his exchange with the Dalton sisters. He could see, in their eyes and in their body language that the angry villagers were readying their pitchforks for the evil day care ogre.

If they thought they could intimidate him, they were wrong. He'd faced far worse, from ego-centric billionaires to feisty CEOs who refused to accept their tenure was done when he bought them out. This small town would be a cakewalk. He'd play their game, make nice, but in the end, he'd do what he always did—

Win.

He got to his feet and turned to face the room. He could handle these people. All he had to do was pretend to be one of them. Charming, gentle, friendly. His last girlfriend had accused him of being the Tin Man, because he didn't have a heart. Maybe she was right. But he could damn well act the part. "Folks, I'm Walker Jones, Hudson's older brother, and yes, the owner of Just Us Kids. I'm here in town to check on things, reassure you all that we run a quality operation. I'd like to take a moment to thank you all for the warm welcome to your lovely town."

Cold eyes stared back at him. One man crossed his arms over his chest and glared at Walker. Another woman shook her head and turned away.

He widened his smile, loosened his stance. As easy and welcoming as a new neighbor. "And I can think of no better way to thank you all for your hospitality than a round on me." A low cheer sounded from the back of the room. Walker smiled and put up a hand. "Now, I know a few beers won't change much, and I don't expect it to. I just want to say thank you. And if any of you have any questions, come on up to the bar. I'd sure like to meet the residents of Rust Creek Falls."

Just as he knew it would, the icy wall between himself and the other patrons began to thaw. A few stepped right up to the bar, giving him a thank-you as they placed their orders.

"I figure it's always a good idea to make friends with the guy buying the beer," said a barrel-chested man with a thick beard and a red flannel shirt. "Elvin Houseman."

"Walker Jones." They shook hands. "Pleased to meet you."

Elvin leaned in close to Walker's ear. "Folks round here are gonna have a hard time trusting you. When those kids got sick over at the day care, it scared a lot of people."

"I'm doing my best to rectify that, Mr. Houseman."

The other man waved that off. "Nobody calls me Mr. Houseman. I'm just Elvin."

"Elvin, then."

Lani slid a beer across to Elvin. He raised it toward

her, then toward Walker. "Thank you kindly. And best
of luck to you with the town." He gave Walker a little
nod, then walked away.

Walker glanced at Lindsay. She'd either ignored or
hadn't noticed the whole exchange. She also hadn't
ordered a fresh drink, not that he expected her to take
advantage of the round on his tab, but clearly, she
wasn't won over like the other folks in the bar, nor
did she seem to be intimidated by him. But there was
a hint of surprise in her face. She clearly hadn't expected him to outflank her by going straight to the
town. Walker headed back to his table.

Before he reached his seat, one of the giggling
blondes who had come in earlier stood in front of
him, her hips swaying to the music. She put her hands
out. "Hey, would you like to dance? Come on, we
need a man."

The blonde was pretty, probably no older than
twenty-three or twenty-four. On any other day, she'd
be the kind of diversion Walker would go for—no
real commitment, nothing expected after the evening
was over. He'd dated enough of that type of woman to
know how it would go—a few drinks, a few laughs, a
good time in bed and then back to real life.

He wanted to say no, to tell her he had enough on
his mind already, but then he reconsidered. Dancing
with the local girl fed into his plan of ingratiating
himself with the town, and would also show Lindsay Dalton an unexpected side of him. He wanted to
keep the other lawyer as off balance as he could. If
she didn't know what to expect from him, the advantage would go to Walker.

So he shrugged off his suit jacket, undid his tie

and the top two buttons of his shirt, then rolled up his shirt sleeves. "Sure."

The blonde giggled again, then grabbed his hand. "It's line dancing. Do you know how to do that?"

"Follow your hips?"

That made her laugh again. "Exactly."

The blonde and her trio of friends surrounded him, and the five of them moved from one side of the dance floor to the other, doing something the girls called a grapevine that they'd learned from that Billy Ray Cyrus video "Achy Breaky Heart." Though he'd never danced like this before, it was fairly simple, and by the time the first verse was finished, Walker had most of the steps memorized.

He had, however, all but forgotten the blonde. His gaze kept straying across the room to Lindsay Dalton, still sitting on the bar stool and chatting with her sister. He watched Lindsay, just to see if his plan was working, he told himself.

He'd done a little research on his opponent in the hours after court. Lindsay Dalton, the youngest of six children, fresh from taking the bar exam and now working for her father's firm. She had been successful with some very small cases she'd argued—a boundary line, something about a dog dispute, those kinds of things. Nothing as big as a lawsuit against a major national corporation, albeit one division of the Jones empire. Yet she hadn't seemed too daunted in the courtroom. If anything, she'd impressed him with her attitude—like a kitten standing up to a tiger.

Though the kitten wouldn't even get to unsheathe its claws at the tiger, her attempt made him respect her. And made him wonder about her.

Across the bar, Lindsay was laughing at something the bartender had said. He liked the sound of her laugh, light and lyrical, and the way it lit her face, put a little dash of a tease into her eyes. He knew he shouldn't—she was the enemy, after all—but he really wanted to get to know her better.

It was research, that was all. Figuring out what made the other side tick so he'd have a better chance in court.

The blonde and her friends circled to the left at the same time that Lindsay started to cross the room. Walker stepped to the right and captured Lindsay's hand. "Dance with me."

Her eyes widened. "Dance...with *you*?"

"Come on." He swayed his hips and swung their arms. She stayed stiff, reluctant. He could hardly blame her. After all, just a few hours ago, they'd been facing off in court. "It's the weekend. Let's forget about court cases and arguments and just..."

"Have fun?" She arched a brow.

He shot her a grin. "I hear they do that, even in towns as small as Rust Creek Falls."

That made her laugh. Her hips were swaying along with his, though she didn't seem to be aware she was moving to the beat. "Are you saying my town is boring?"

Boring? She had no idea. But he wouldn't tell her that. Instead he gave her his patented killer smile. "I'm saying it's a small town. With some great music on the juke and a dance floor just waiting for you." He lifted her hand and spun her to the right, then back out again to the left. "Come on, Ms. Dalton, dance with me. Me, the man, not me, the corporation you're suing."

"I shouldn't..." She started to slide her hand out of his.

He stepped closer to her. "Shouldn't have fun? Shouldn't dance with the enemy?"

"I shouldn't do anything with the enemy."

He grinned, to show her he wasn't all bad. Keep her on her toes, keep her from predicting him, and keep the advantage on his side. "I'm not asking for anything. Just a dance."

Another song came on the juke, and the blonde and her friends started up again, moving from one side of the dance floor to the other. Their movements swept Walker and Lindsay into the middle of the dance floor, leaving her with two choices—dance with him or wade through the other women to escape.

For a second, he thought he'd won and she was going to dance with him. Then the smile on her face died, and she shook her head. "I'm sorry, Mr. Jones, but I don't dance with people who don't take responsibility for their mistakes."

Then she turned on her heel and left the dance floor and a moment later, the bar.

Walker tried to muster up some enthusiasm to dance with the other women—any man in his right mind would have taken that opportunity—but he couldn't. He excused himself, paid his tab then left the bar. The victories he'd had today in court and later in the bar rang hollow in the cool night air.

Lindsay headed home, her stomach still in knots. She rolled down the driver side window of her sedan, letting in the fresh, crisp October Montana air, and tried to appreciate the clear, blank landscape ahead of her and the bright stars in the sky. But her mind kept going back to Walker Jones, to that moment in the bar.

Had she almost danced with him?

What was she thinking? He was the enemy, the one responsible for little baby Georgina's illness and scary hospital stay. Maybe not him personally, but his company, and the lack of standards at his day care centers, was indeed responsible. Not to mention how many of her letters and phone calls to Jones's corporate headquarters had gone unanswered, as he clearly tried to ignore the problem or hoped it would go away. He'd been aware of the problem from the minute the outbreak happened in town, and yet he had done nothing. Hadn't flown in to check on the day care, hadn't responded to the worried parents.

She had no interest in Walker Jones. No interest at all. And that little moment in the bar when he'd asked her to dance had been an anomaly, nothing more.

Walker Jones thought he could buy her town through alcohol and joining in on a few line dances. Well, he could think again. Neither she nor Rust Creek Falls would be so easily swayed by that man.

Lindsay headed into the ranch house where she'd grown up. She'd come back home to live after law school, partly because she needed to save money and partly because she'd missed her family. Now it was just her, her brother Travis and their parents. The house didn't ring with the same noise as it did when Lindsay was young, but it still felt like home whenever she walked in the door.

The scents of fresh-baked bread, some kind of deliciousness the family had earlier for dinner and her mother's floral perfume filled the air. It was late, and her parents would have already gone to bed, but Lindsay saw a light on in the kitchen.

"Hey, Trav," she said to her brother as she entered the room. "What has you home early?"

Travis was the one who was known for partying late, dating a new girl every week and living a little wilder than the rest of the Daltons. She adored her brother, but hoped he'd settle down one of these days. He was a good guy, and in Lindsay's opinion, there were far too few of those in the world.

"My date canceled. She got the flu. Didn't feel like heading to the Ace, and so here I am." He crossed to the fridge and pulled open the door. "Plus I heard Mom made meat loaf for dinner."

Lindsay laughed. "I knew it had to be something bigger than a date canceling."

"Hey, I don't get my favorite dinner often enough." He gave her the lopsided grin that had charmed dozens of women over the years. "Want a meat loaf sandwich?"

"Nah, I'm good. I was just going to grab a glass of wine and head out to the back deck. It's a nice night." Hundreds of thoughts and worries jockeyed for space in her mind. She needed some fresh air, some open space. The soft nicker of the horses in the stable, the whisper of a breeze across her face. Not the confines of the kitchen.

Travis handed her the open bottle of chardonnay from the refrigerator door. "Wine on a weeknight? Must have been a hell of a bad day."

"It's Friday night, so technically it's the weekend." She didn't mention that she'd already had a couple of glasses at the Ace in the Hole. Nor did she admit Travis might be right.

"Yeah, right. You, little sister, are about as wild as a house cat lying in the sun." He grinned, then started assembling his sandwich. A thick slice of meat loaf on top of some homemade white bread, then ketchup and a second slice. "Except when you were dating Jeremy back in college and thinking about running off to the big city."

The two of them walked out to the back deck and sat in the Adirondack chairs that faced the wide expanse of the ranch. In the dark, it seemed like the Dalton land stretched forever. The sight was calming, reassuring. "I never thought about running off to the big city," Lindsay said. "That was Jeremy's idea."

Her former fiancé had been smart and witty and driven. She'd met him in law school and liked him from the start. Then, as they neared graduation, he'd told her he had no intentions of living in Montana. He wanted to move to New York and practice law in a place that made him feel alive. For Lindsay, life was here, in the rich soil, the graceful mountains, the clean air. She never wanted to live anywhere else.

"You know, I still keep in touch with old Jer," Travis said. He'd met her fiancé on a visit to see Lindsay, and they'd become fast friends. "He did move to New York. Doing pretty well up there and working in corporate law."

Lindsay sat back against the chair and looked up at the stars dotting the night sky. "I'm glad for him. I really am."

"And over him?"

She cast a curious glance in Travis's direction. "Yeah. But why are you asking? You have that tone."

"What tone?" He gave her an *I'm innocent* look, the one he'd perfected when he was a kid and always in trouble for breaking a vase or missing curfew. Their mother usually just laughed and let Travis off with an easy punishment.

"The one that says you want to convince me to do something crazy." When she'd been younger, she'd gone along with Travis's ideas—camping overnight by a stream, climbing a tree, catching frogs. But their paths had diverged as she grew up and went to college and Travis...

Well, he went on being Travis. Lovable but irresponsible.

"Last I heard, you almost did do something crazy," her brother said. "A little bird—or in my case, a little blonde college coed I used to date—texted and told me you were dancing with a stranger at the Ace tonight. She was a tiny bit jealous, because, in her exact words, 'I had that man first.'"

Lindsay blew her bangs out of her face. "These are the moments when I do wish I lived in a big city. Geesh, does everyone in Rust Creek Falls know how I spent my Friday night? And for your information, I wasn't dancing with him. He asked, and I said no."

Well, sort of said no. There'd been a moment there when she'd been swaying to the music. She'd been tempted, too tempted, to slip into Walker Jones's arms and swing around that dance floor.

"You should have said yes." Travis got to his feet and gathered up his empty plate. He paused at the door and turned back to face her. "You're a great lawyer, sis. Smarter than half the people I know. But you don't take enough risks, don't get your hands dirty often enough. Life is about jumping in with both feet, not standing on the edge and dipping in a toe from time to time."

Jumping in with both feet was foolhardy and risky, two things Lindsay normally shied away from. But for a moment on that dance floor tonight, she'd been both.

She sipped at the wine and watched the stars, so bright and steady in the sky, and told herself there was nothing wrong with being a calm house cat sitting in the sun. Because in the end, that house cat didn't make foolish choices that brought her far too close to enemy lines.

Chapter Three

Walker watched his brother polish off two plates of eggs and a pile of crispy bacon before he launched into a teetering pile of pancakes. Walker had stuck to a couple pieces of toast and some coffee, his usual breakfast choice. He'd never been much of a morning eater, but his brother Hudson—he could eat all day and still be hungry at bedtime.

The food and accommodations at Maverick Manor, where Walker had decided to stay last night, were outstanding. When he'd spent a night here a few months ago, he'd been surprised. He'd expected something more…primitive, given the size of Rust Creek Falls, but the two-story log cabin–style resort rivaled any five-star hotel Walker had stayed at before. Owned by a local, Nate Crawford, the resort showed the love Nate had for the place at every turn. It had wrap-around porches, big windows in every room and expansive views of the beautiful Montana landscape. He'd almost felt like he was staying in a tree house when he woke up this morning—if a tree house was big enough to hold one of the comfiest king-size beds Walker had ever slept in. The rooms were filled with overstuffed, comfortable furniture, all decorated in natural hues of beige and brown, the perfect complement to the log walls.

There'd been a copy of *The Rust Creek Falls Gazette*, the local paper, outside his door, filled with the usual small-town stuff—birth announcements, cows for sale, missing pickup trucks. It was all hokey stuff, making him wonder if these people were either a town full of Pollyannas or simply immune to the real world, where the front-page story wasn't about a prize mare giving birth to twin foals.

Either way, Walker wanted to leave Rust Creek Falls as quickly as possible. The whole place grated on his nerves. The sooner he got back to Tulsa and the day-to-day operations of his business, the better, which meant not delaying the reason for this meeting, even for pancakes.

"Let's talk about the day care," Walker said. He waved off the waitress's offer of more coffee.

Hudson pushed his empty plate to the side, then wiped his mouth with a napkin. "Things are going great."

"As in, you're there every day and are verifying that with your own eyes?"

Hudson shrugged, avoided Walker's gaze. "Well, yeah, more or less."

Walker's shoulders tensed. He'd trusted his

brother—and had thought it was a mistake from the start. But his father had said it would be a good idea to give Hudson a piece of the family business. Get him more involved, more invested, before their father stepped down entirely. This past year, his father had put Walker in the CEO position, while his dad took on the role of Chairman of the Board. The elder Jones continued to leave his fingerprints all over the company, as if he was still in charge. Walker hoped that once both he and his brother were part of the company, their father would ease up. But thus far, Hudson hadn't displayed the same love for business. Hudson was a good man, a hard worker, but clearly had no desire to be involved with the family business like Walker did. Maybe Walker had read his brother wrong, and made a mistake involving him in the day care franchise.

Walker leased the building from Hudson, who owned the land it sat on. Walker had hired Bella to be a part-time manager, expecting Hudson to fill in the gaps. "What does *more or less* mean?"

"Place pretty much runs itself. Besides, Bella, the manager, is one of those people who likes to keep things in line, so I let her." Hudson took a long swig of coffee.

"Hudson, you bought this property—"

"As an investment." Hudson shrugged again. "You know, pocket money."

Walker bit back his frustration. He should have known his brother would let him down. Their father had hoped, when Walker leased the building on the land Hudson bought, that his brother would actually get involved in the family business. As a fail safe, Walker had hired Bella, hoping she'd serve as Hudson's right hand. Every time Walker had asked Hudson how things were going, his brother had said everything was fine. Implying he was there every day. Now, it turned out that Hudson was off...being Hudson.

"When are you going to grow up, Hudson? Take some responsibility, for once, instead of going from job to job, place to place? Actually settle down?"

"What, like you? Work twelve million hours a week and never date because you don't have time to do anything other than—surprise—work?" Hudson shook his head. "No, thank you. I like to have a life."

"I have a life."

Hudson snorted.

"And just because I work a lot doesn't mean I don't get out, go on trips, date—"

"Name the last time you did any of the above."

Why was Walker feeling so damned defensive? It had to be the small town, which had him out of his element and out of his normal moods. "I went to the Ace in the Hole last night and did some line dancing."

Hudson's brown brows arched. He was a younger version of Walker, with the same facial expressions. "Are you serious? For real?" Hudson said.

"Yes, for real. I'm not all work and no play," he argued. Although Hudson was right. The last time Walker had done anything like that was so far in the distant past, he couldn't even remember it. When he was in Tulsa, his days blurred into a constant hamster wheel of work, work and more work. There were deals to be made, holdings to oversee, marketing to develop, accounting reports to analyze. Jones Holdings, Inc., was so diversified that Walker constantly felt like he was playing catch-up. He didn't have room in his life for anything other than work.

Or at least that was what he told himself. He had a great team working for him, and if he really wanted to, he could take time off. Go on vacation. Pick up a hobby.

Date.

Except he hadn't had a relationship that lasted more than a couple nights in more than two years. Not since Theresa had ended their five-year relationship, saying she wanted a man who invested his heart, not just his bank account.

Walker still didn't know what she meant by that. He'd given her everything he could, or thought he had. The lines had been blurred, though, because Theresa had worked for him, and more often than not, their date night conversations had been about work. She'd wanted more romance, she told him, more of his heart.

He'd told her he wasn't sure he had a heart to give. Work had been his passion for so long, he didn't know any other way to live. Eventually Theresa had given up on him and moved on. Last he heard, she had married an accountant and was expecting their first child. There were days when Walker wondered if maybe he'd missed out on something great. But those moments only lasted a second, because he was smart enough to know he was happiest when he was at work.

Once again Lindsay Dalton sprang into his mind. She was the kind of woman, Walker was sure, who would want the romance and the kids and the house with a yard. She might be all business in the courtroom, but he sensed a softness about her, a sentimentality, when she smiled. When she'd been talking to her sister. And when she'd started to dance.

That had made him wonder just how much fun Lindsay was trying to hide beneath those courtroom suits.

"Back to the day care," Walker said, done with thinking about and discussing his personal life. A few days here, and he'd be back to the daily grind. He'd be happier in Tulsa. Less distracted by things like Lindsay Dalton's smile lingering in his mind. "There's a lot of ill will toward Just Us Kids because of this lawsuit. In order to expand the business, I need to turn the tide here in Rust Creek Falls. Even if we win the lawsuit, there are still going to be people who will believe the day care caused that illness. I want to head off the negative publicity from the get-go."

"Something you're apparently already doing," Hudson said. "I heard you bought everyone a round last night."

"How'd you hear about that?"

Hudson grinned. "It's a small town. Everyone knows everything here." He took a sip of coffee, then forked up a forgotten last bite of pancake. "If you want to build goodwill here, the best thing you can do is something that gets you involved with the town. One thing about Rust Creek Falls—it's like a big family. They'll accept you as one of their own—"

"You make it sound like an ant colony. Or the Borg."

Hudson laughed. "Pretty close. I never expected to like this place, but you know, living out on Clive Barker's ranch property and coming into town from time to time…it's started to grow on me. It might do the same for you."

Walker scoffed. "I'm leaving the minute this lawsuit is concluded. Until then, all I'm focused on is winning."

"The lawsuit and the hearts and minds?" Hudson asked.

"All part of the strategy," Walker said.

Hudson sighed. "Why did I ever think five minutes of dancing meant you were becoming human?"

Walker didn't dignify that with an answer. If his brother focused more on business and less on having fun, then maybe Hudson would understand.

"You know, Walker, I'm not this irresponsible screwup you keep making me out to be," Hudson said.

"Then what are you doing with your days instead of overseeing the day care?"

"Going back and forth between here and Wyoming, helping a friend set up a horse ranch. I'm helping him hire people, implement a solid record keeping system, buying the horses…in other words, running a business."

Walker was impressed, but kept that thought to himself. He didn't want to encourage his brother to spend time in Wyoming, not with this lawsuit on their backs. "I'd rather you were running the day care here."

Hudson rolled his eyes. "There is no pleasing you, is there? Can't you start thinking about something outside the family business for five minutes?"

"That family business puts the money in your bank account to do this horse ranch thing. If you were smart, you'd be helping me protect it, not beating me up for not having more fun."

Hudson drummed his fingers on the table for a moment, then sighed. "Okay, if you want to make people like you, do something nice for the town. Something hands-on. This isn't the kind of place that's going to appreciate a bunch of money thrown at it."

Walker scowled. "I wasn't going to do any such thing." Truth be told, he'd thought maybe he could just make a sizable donation to the local community center or a food bank or something and be done with it. He could see Hudson's point. A round of beers only bought temporary goodwill. He needed something bigger. Something involved. Something...

An orange flyer stuffed in the small plastic tabletop sign holder caught his eye.

Rust Creek Falls Harvest Festival!
Get involved now and help make this year's festival the best ever!

The announcement was followed by an invitation for volunteers to meet at the local high school Saturday afternoon. Today.

"Here's something I can do," he said to his brother, spinning the sign toward Hudson.

Hudson laughed. "You? Help with the harvest festival? Have you ever even attended a festival?"

"Doesn't matter. All I have to do is pitch in with... whatever they do to put together one of these things. People will see I care about the town. Problem solved."

Hudson sat back and gave his brother a dubious look. "You honestly think it's going to be as easy as that? This is real life, big brother. It's not some report you analyze or an interview you do with some overly enthusiastic CPA."

"And it's not rocket science, either." Walker dropped some bills on the table, leaving a generous tip for the waitress. "You stay in town for a while this time. Get to work at the day care and make sure the place is so clean and neat, no kid would get sick if he licked the floor. When they call you into court—and I'm sure they will, since you are the landlord—you can honestly say you saw that the place was in order. I'll stop in later, after I check out this festival thing." He picked up the flyer and tucked it in his pocket. "This might just be step one in my campaign to not only beat Lindsay Dalton but build the Just Us Kids chain."

And that would get him out of this town, back to work and away from women who lingered in his thoughts for all the wrong reasons.

Travis had been right. Getting hands-on was a nice change, Lindsay thought as she stacked wood in a pile to start building the vendor booths for the harvest festival. There weren't that many volunteers here today, probably because a lot of people were at the craft fair at the church. The handful of people in the gymnasium had divvied up the various jobs as best they could, but even Lindsay could see they were going to be shorthanded. She didn't mind, really. She'd been spending so much time in the office, working on the court case, that it felt good to do something constructive. Something that didn't also raise her blood pressure because it went with thinking about Walker

Jones. Yes, a little construction project today would be a good distraction, on all levels.

Lani came by, with Russ at her side. The two of them looked so blissfully happy that Lindsay felt a flicker of envy. What would it be like to have someone look at her like that? To take her hand, just because, then smile at her like she was the most precious thing on earth?

"Hey, sis, we're heading out with the landscaping volunteers to do some work in the park. There's a tree that needs to come down and some shrubbery that needs to be pruned." Lani gestured toward the wood. "Are you going to work on that by yourself?"

"I think I can handle a few simple booths." Lindsay flexed a biceps. "I have skills."

Russ laughed. "You sure you don't want one of us to stay and help you?"

"No, no, I've got it. The outdoor work is important. If that doesn't get done, there won't be any place to put the booths." Lindsay picked up the cordless drill and pressed the button. It whirred and spun. There, that should make her look confident. The booths, after all, were pretty much just oversize squares. "I can do this with my eyes closed."

"Okay. We should be back in a couple hours. If you need anything, holler." Lani gave Lindsay a quick hug, then the two of them headed out the door.

Lindsay propped her hands on her hips and looked at the pile of wood. She had a rudimentary sketch, given to her by Sam Traven, co-owner of the Ace in the Hole, of what the booths should look like. A box base, with a long flat piece of plywood to serve as a table, then a frame above it to hang signage from. Like a child's lemonade stand, only bigger.

She had a cordless drill, wood screws and precut wood. What she didn't have was a clue of how to put this together. Okay, so maybe she'd been a little too optimistic when she told Lani and Russ she could handle this.

Lindsay picked up a two-by-four, then one of the shorter pieces. It seemed like this shorter piece should create the sides, then connect to another shorter piece, then another longer one... Okay, one piece at a time. It was just a big box, right?

She put the longest piece on the floor, then got out a wood screw and let the magnetic end of the drill bit connect to it. She knelt beside the two pieces, then tried to hold the shorter one in place while she drilled the screw into it and connected them.

Or tried to. Turned out that holding a piece of wood with her left hand while trying to operate the cordless drill with her right hand was a whole lot harder than they made it look on *Fix or Flip*. The screw whined, twirled into the wood, but refused to go straight, leaving the whole connection askew. Lindsay brushed her bangs off her forehead, then flipped the switch on the drill and tried to back the screw out. It whined and spun but didn't pull back.

"It works a lot better if you use a little pressure," said a deep voice behind her.

Lindsay sighed and rocked back on her heels. "Thanks. Do you mind help—" She cut off her words when she realized who belonged to the voice.

Walker Jones III.

Great. The last person she wanted to see. He

was like a mangy dog, turning up in the least likely places, at the worst possible times. "What are you doing here?"

He nodded toward the wood pile. "Same as you. Helping with the harvest festival."

She scoffed. "Right. And why the heck would you do that?"

"To build goodwill." He shrugged. "I want people in this town to like me. So sue me. Oh, wait, you already are."

At least he was honest about why he was here. But that didn't make her like the idea any more. She wanted Walker Jones gone from Rust Creek Falls, gone from her peripheral vision…just gone. Even if he did looked damned good in jeans and a white button-down shirt with the cuffs rolled up. "You just want to win the lawsuit. Buying a round of beers and helping set up for a harvest festival won't do that."

"Walker Jones?" Rosey Traven, Sam's wife and the other co-owner of the Ace in the Hole, came striding over. She reached out and took his hand, giving him a hearty shake. "I heard you were in my bar last night, buying beers for everyone. That was a really nice thing to do."

"Thank you, ma'am," he said, shaking Rosey's hand as he spoke. "I figured since I was new in town, I should say thank you for the warm welcome I received."

Warm welcome? Lindsay rolled her eyes.

"Well, there's no better way to say thank you than with a couple of drinks." Rosey smiled, then turned to Lindsay. "Hi, Lindsay. Nice to see you here today. We sure appreciate your help with the booths."

"You're welcome. I'm glad to help." She pointed at the convoluted boards. "Once I figure out how, that is."

"You've got some handsome help here. I'm sure he can figure out how to get that together right quick." Rosey smiled at Walker. "I best be going. Sam and I are bringing sandwiches to all the volunteers in the park. You two have fun!"

Which left Lindsay alone with Walker. Again. "Listen, we are on two different sides of a lawsuit," she said, trying to work the drill again and back out the screw. It whined and groaned in place. "Damn it!"

"You're going to strip the screw. Let me help you." Walker's hand covered hers.

She didn't want to like his touch. Didn't want to react. But her body didn't listen to her head. The second his hand connected with hers, his larger fingers encompassing her smaller ones, a little flutter ran through her veins. In that instant, she was acutely aware of how close he was. How good he smelled. How the veins in his hands extended up his muscular forearms.

And how much she wanted to kiss him.

"I've got it." She yanked the drill up, so fast and so hard that it sent her sprawling back. That flutter had been an anomaly. That was all.

Walker's hand was there again, stopping her from hitting the floor. A quick touch, but it sent another explosion through her veins. "Whoa. I said a little pressure. Not a tidal wave."

"I can handle this. I don't need your help." It was a lie—she needed help—but she didn't want it from the man she had sworn to hate. The same man who was—damn it—handsome. And intriguing.

"How many things have you built?" Walker said.

"None." She waved that answer off. "But I can read directions."

"That's great, except some things come with experience, not directions." Walker gestured toward the misassembled corner. "You are a smart, capable, beautiful woman, but you are tearing up that screw head and making it almost impossible to take those two pieces apart. Now, you may not want my help, but I think you need it, at least for a minute."

Had he just called her beautiful? Why did a part of her do a little giddy dance at that?

Lindsay bent her head and worked on the screw again, but the two pieces of wood were not coming apart. The screw refused to go anywhere but in a pointless circle. Lindsay really didn't know what to do with a stripped screw head, or what one even was, only that it sounded bad. She was going to mess this up, and that would mean someone would have to buy more wood. For a festival that was operating on a shoestring budget to begin with, that would be a disaster, and Lindsay didn't want that on her shoulders. She knew when she was beaten, even if the victor was some scraps of wood and a single screw.

She handed him the drill. "Fine. You do it."

To his credit, Walker didn't say *I told you so*. He held the pieces firmly with one hand, pressed the drill into the screw and let the bit whir slowly as he backed the screw out a little at a time. Clearly, the key was patience and pressure.

Pretty much the same thing in a court case, Lindsay

thought. A lot of patience and a little pressure usually equaled success.

"Thanks," she said. The two pieces of wood were still intact, though the screw was worse for wear. Far better to replace one screw than the more expensive wood, which was still fine to use. "I'll admit, I'm impressed."

Walker chuckled. "I can't build a house or anything, but I do have some handyman skills. My grandpa liked to make things, and I was at his house most weekends when I was a kid, so he taught me what he could." His gaze went to someplace far away. Dwelling on memories, perhaps? "I miss him terribly, and every time I see a birdhouse, it makes me think of him. He was a hell of a guy."

She hated that a simple story about his grandpa could make her see him in a different light. She wanted to hate Walker Jones III and his evil empire for how it had mismanaged the Just Us Kids Day Care. Except that was hard to do that when Walker got all sentimental talking about building a birdhouse. "That's...sweet."

"You say it like you're surprised."

"Maybe I am a little." Okay, a lot. For two months, she'd been sending letters and leaving messages for this faceless evil man in a corporate office. But now that Walker was here and in the flesh, she couldn't quite muster up the same feelings of animosity.

"I can tell what you're thinking. I'm not this horrible corporate monster who only cares about the bottom line, you know." He picked up the next piece of wood. "In fact, let me prove it to you."

"Prove it to me? How?"

He waved the wood at her, then grabbed a handful of screws. "Let me help you construct these."

Working all day side by side with Walker Jones? Having him distract her and make her forget that he was the enemy, not a man she wanted to kiss? Lindsay shook her head. "I don't think that's a good idea. I'm suing you, and we shouldn't be talking to each other."

"For one, you're suing my company, not me personally. And for another, as long as we don't talk about the day care or the lawsuit, we should be just fine." He put out his hand. "Deal?"

She hesitated. She knew she shouldn't work with him, especially not with the pending lawsuit, but there were few people in the room, and all these booths to build, and given her track record so far, there wasn't much chance that Lindsay could build them herself. And maybe if she spent some time with Walker she could figure out what made him tick—and use that to her advantage in the courtroom next week.

"Deal." She shook with him, and that same zing ran through her. Clearly, it wasn't an anomaly. Which meant Lindsay might just be making an incredibly big mistake.

But then Walker let her go and started talking about the best method of assembling the booths, and she realized he must not have felt the same jolt. He was being detached and businesslike and doing exactly what he'd promised to do—helping. She had nothing to worry about, as long as she could keep herself in check. Which she could easily do, she told herself.

"Okay, so this piece goes here?" she said, picking up another short one. Work on the booth and forget about the way his touch had seared her skin, yup, that was the plan.

"I'll hold it together. You'll drill a pilot hole first, then sink the screw."

"Me? Drill a what?"

"Here, change out the bit to a drill bit." He showed her how to loosen the chuck then slip in the new bit and tighten it again. "If you drill a pilot hole, it keeps the screw from putting as much pressure on the wood and you have less chance of splitting the wood."

She did as he instructed, using just enough pressure to drill the narrow pilot hole, then back out the bit and change it out for a Phillips head. She poised herself over the two pieces of wood, a little hesitant. "And now we try this again. You sure you have a good hold on it?"

"It'll be fine. Just remember to go slow and keep even pressure on the drill."

She did as he said, and when the screw sank into place, Walker let go. The two sides of the booth held together, perfectly perpendicular. "I did it."

Walker grinned. "You did. Great job."

Confidence filled her chest. Maybe this wasn't such an impossible project. Of course, she was only on the first booth, but still… "Can we do the next piece?"

He chuckled. "Yup. Same idea as before. Ready?"

She grabbed another screw, then hoisted the cordless drill. Right now, she felt like a superhero. She had only built a tiny portion of one booth—with Walker's help—but there was something deeply satisfying about building anything with her own hands that gave her a sudden burst of self-assurance. "Yup."

"You do a mighty good impression of Bob Vila," he said, "only you are way prettier than him."

That made her laugh and flushed her cheeks. Twice now he'd complimented her on her looks. But she told herself the words meant nothing, and she should take his remarks in stride. "I should hope so," she said, laughing them off. "Though if I grow a beard, we might up end up looking like twins."

"Trust me. No one would ever mistake you for Bob Vila."

"Thanks." She ducked her head, hoping he hadn't seen how the flattery pleased her, despite her resolve. Or how tempted she was to keep looking into his blue eyes.

They worked together for a few minutes. Walker was a patient, easygoing teacher who coached her from time to time and made the whole process ten times less stressful. He held the pieces while she connected them, the two of them falling into an easy, unspoken rhythm. They would bump up against each other occasionally or just be within a few inches of each other. Every time he brushed up against her, her heart did a little flutter flip. And then her head scolded her for her reaction.

Soon as the booths were built, she was going to put some distance between herself and Walker. This... attraction she felt for him would lead nowhere good.

In almost no time at all, they had framed the first booth. "Let's get that plywood on," Walker said. He hoisted the heavy piece into place, then handed her the drill. "Just screw down each of the corners, and then we'll put a few more screws along the longer sides to give it more stability."

She did as he said, but her focus kept sputtering. She was acutely aware of the muscles in his hands, the dark scent of his cologne, the broad expanse of his chest and how very, very good he looked in jeans. "There. I think we're done."

They both stepped back and took a second to admire their work. The booth stood tall and straight and ready for business. A sense of pride washed over Lindsay. "We did it."

"We did." He turned to her and smiled. "Seems we *can* work together for the common good."

She laughed. "Don't get used to it."

"Trust me, I won't." He waved toward the pile of wood, and the teasing mood evaporated. They were back to all business about the booths. "How many more to go?"

"Nine." She perched her fists on her hips. The pile of wood seemed awfully high, and the number of hours left to work awfully low. As much as she wanted to get rid of Walker so she would stop noticing his hands and his cologne, she knew she couldn't finish this job on her own. "Think we can do it?"

"Are you inviting me to stay and help?"

Was she? All she knew was that she had a lot of booths to build and working with Walker wasn't as bad as she'd expected. She might even call it…enjoyable, if she was feeling charitable. "Turns out you're kind of handy to have around, Walker Jones." She wagged a finger at him. "Just don't expect any of this to influence how I go after you in court next week."

"Still a bulldog, huh?"

"Of course."

He grinned again. "I wouldn't want it any other way, Ms. Dalton."

"Me, neither," she said, then turned to the next booth. Because the last thing she needed was to let down her defenses and fall for the man who was going to be sitting on the opposite side of the courtroom in a few days.

Chapter Four

Walker hadn't planned on it. Not at all. But it happened. He liked Lindsay Dalton. She was beautiful and funny and smart, but most of all, determined. He liked that best about her. The way she didn't back down from a challenge, didn't find a task too daunting. They were traits that would serve her well in court—

Which was a definite disadvantage to him.

If he was smart, he'd steer clear of her. In fact, every part of his brain was telling him to walk away. Right now. But something kept him there, even as he fed himself the fiction that he was merely trying to gain a better understanding of the opposing side, as part of maintaining his edge over her. So he kept on building the booths with her, one after another, like an assembly line of wood and screws.

But every time she got within a few inches of him, his entire body went on high alert.

Yeah, he was attracted to her. Very much so. He kept trying to pretend all he was here for was building the booths and good community relations and researching the opposing counsel, but really, he'd stopped caring about the festival a long time ago. All he wanted was more time with Lindsay.

"So, did you grow up around here?" he asked.

She arched a brow. "Is this small talk or investigating the opposing counsel?"

She was smart, too, and he'd do well to remember that before he got tripped up on his own plan.

"Neither." He sat back on his heels. "I'm interested in you. Genuinely interested."

She opened her mouth. Closed it again. "We can't… I mean, we shouldn't…"

"I'm not asking you to marry me, Lindsay. Just whether you grew up around here." It was the first time he'd used her given name, and it rolled off his tongue with ease. A little flare of surprise lit her eyes, which told him she'd noticed the name, too. He'd done it only to gain an edge, no other reason.

"And just because I answer your questions doesn't mean I want to marry you, either," she said.

He laughed. "Is everything with you an argument?"

That made a grin quirk up one corner of her mouth. "My mother would say I was born ready to argue."

"My mother said the same thing about me. She used to say I'd argue about the color of the sky on a cloudy day. I was the difficult one, according to her."

"Hmm…" Lindsay put a finger to her lips. "I might have to agree with that opinion."

"Ah, but you hardly know me." He leaned in closer to her, and against his better judgment, inhaled the sweet scent of her perfume, watched the tick of her pulse in her neck. "I'm not as bad as I seem on paper."

"Maybe you're much worse."

He could tell that it was going to take a whole lot more than some beer and booths to impress the lawyer. She was a challenge, and if there was one thing Walker loved, it was a challenge. "Just give me a chance, that's all I ask."

"It won't change anything, Mr. Jones. I'm still taking you to court."

"I wouldn't expect anything less from you." He connected the next two pieces, then tried again. Reminded himself he was here to get to know her, as an opponent, nothing else. "So...did you grow up around here?"

She laughed this time. "You don't give up easily, do you?"

"I suspect neither do you."

"You've got that right." She handed him the next board, then jiggled a few screws in her palm. "Yes, I did grow up here. The Dalton family is as much a part of Rust Creek Falls as the earth the town sits on. I went away for college and law school, and for a brief time, I thought about moving to the city once I got my JD, but I love it here. It's...home."

A soft, sentimental smile swept across her face. Her eyes took on a dreamy sheen. Walker almost felt... jealous.

He'd never loved anything or anyplace as much as Lindsay Dalton clearly loved this town. What would it be like to come home to a place like that? To feel like you belonged?

In that cold, perfect museum his parents had called a home, he had never felt like he belonged. With his father judging everything he said and did, and his mother involved in every cause but her own children, Walker had hated his childhood home. His brothers were the only thing that had made it tolerable. When he'd gone to his grandfather's, where life was simple and the rules were light, he'd felt happy. Like he was meant to be there, building things in the garage his grandfather had turned into a woodshop. The way Lindsay talked about Rust Creek Falls made him think of the scent of his grandfather's cologne, the way the woodsy smell blended with the scent of wood shavings. That gravelly voice giving him wisdom about life and girls, while the sandpaper *scritched* along a plank of wood.

Damn. Now he was getting all sentimental. If there was one thing Walker had learned, it was that sentimentality didn't mix with business. Or lawsuits.

"So what about you?" she asked. "Did you grow up in Tulsa?"

"Nope. In a nearby city, Jenks. My family has never been the small-town type and neither have I. Honestly, I have no idea how people live in a place like this. It's so…claustrophobic."

"Then why open a business here?"

"It made sense on paper." He shrugged. "There are few child care options in the immediate area, it's centrally located and can draw from other towns, and the building needed minimal changes to convert it to a day care."

She looked skeptical. "In other words, the entire decision was based on numbers, not emotions?"

"Is there another way to make decisions?" Walker said. "I'm not going to run my business based on how cute Main Street is." He put a sarcastic emphasis on the cute.

"I'm not talking about cuteness," Lindsay said, her hackles up, fire in her eyes. "But when you open a business in a place like this, you have to realize that it's not just another storefront in a row of strip malls. Any business that operates in Rust Creek Falls becomes part of the fabric of the community."

He scoffed. "Fabric of the community? This is a business, not a knitting circle."

As soon as he said the words, he realized he was undermining his goal of pretending to be one of the people of Rust Creek Falls. If he let his disdain for small-town life show, everything he'd done so far would be undone. "But this town seems like a really great place to live."

"It is," she said. "You'll see that if you stay here for a few days."

I doubt that highly. "I'm sure I will." He gave her a smile that he hoped said he wasn't the evil small-town-hating ogre she thought he was. "I guess I'm a little out of touch with what it's like to live here. I live a couple miles from the corporate headquarters in Tulsa." He didn't add that he would bet a thousand dollars that Lindsay lived in some kind of homey place with a wide front porch, the diametric opposite to his fifteenth-floor apartment decorated in glass and chrome. Everything about this town seemed like something out of an episode of *Little House on the*

Prairie, except with the modern conveniences of electricity and wireless phones.

They worked for a little while, the conversation falling into a lull.

"So, is it just you and your brothers?" she asked after they assembled another booth. "Autry, Gideon and...Jensen, right? And I've seen Hudson around town now and then."

She'd done her homework. "Yes. Even though I have a bunch of brothers, my parents weren't exactly... parentish," he said. "My dad worked a lot and my mother was involved in her charities. We were more often with the nanny than with them."

"That's...awful."

"It's a childhood. We all have one." He shrugged, like it didn't matter.

"I grew up on a ranch," Lindsay said as she held the two legs of the booth together and waited for him to attach them to the brace. "Horses, pastures, big family dinners, the whole nine yards. I still live there now, just while I'm establishing my career."

He finished the next booth and reached for the plywood countertop to install. "I couldn't imagine living with anyone in my family. Working with my father is more than enough together time. He can be a little... hardheaded."

Hardheaded was putting it mildly. Walker Jones II had high expectations for all his sons, but he reserved the highest for his namesake. Walker had done his best to live up to that family mantle, but the times when he had tried to go his own way, his father had lectured him like he was two years old again. The older Walker got, the more he butted heads with his father, over everything from the type of coffee in the conference room to the directions the corporation should take going forward. His phone buzzed all day with texts and emails from his father—which Walker did his best to ignore. As he reminded his father often, Walker was a grown-up who didn't need to be ordered around. But his father rarely listened—to anyone.

Lindsay laughed. "Hmm... Jones family trait?"

"Maybe." She had a really sweet, musical laugh. For a millisecond, he forgot she was the opposing counsel.

He'd done that at the courthouse on Friday, too. When he'd seen her with the baby, he'd seen a softer side, a gentler dimension to the no-nonsense lawyer. There'd also been a degree of tension between them, ever since they started working side by side. Half of him wanted to kiss her—and half of him thought he should back away before he got even more connected to the one woman who wanted to ruin him.

He stood and turned and realized they were out of plywood. This was it, he told himself. His opportunity to leave. So why was he not moving? It was if his feet weren't listening to his brain.

"We'll need a few more sheets to finish up the last few booths," Walker said. "Do you know where the supplies are?"

Where did those words come from? He was supposed to be leaving!

She nodded. "Everything's being stored in that room behind the gym. Four pieces of plywood is a lot to carry, so maybe I should come help you."

Oh, that wasn't good. It meant she'd be spending more time with him, even if it was only the few minutes it took to get the plywood. Being alone with her was definitely not a good idea. But he didn't say no.

They crossed the gym, with her leading the way. She had on jeans and a T-shirt, her hair back in a ponytail again. She looked like the kind of woman who curled up on the couch at the end of the day with a movie or a book. It was so foreign to Walker's life. His evenings were often spent reading reports or answering emails or analyzing financial data. He couldn't remember the last time he'd watched more than ten minutes of television.

In many ways, Lindsay was like Theresa, who had complained about how much he worked, and talked about wanting a home with a fence and a dog. That wasn't the life he led, or the life he wanted.

His attraction to Lindsay was irrelevant. The only thing he needed to worry about was winning the court case.

"Back here," Lindsay said, opening a door at the back of the room. It led down a darkened hallway and into a second room on the right. She patted the wall. "The light switch should be right…here. Somewhere…"

She patted the wall some more. Then turned at the same time he did. They collided in the dark space, skin against skin, her head landing just under his chin, her curves pressed against his chest. "I… I can't find the light switch," she said.

Was she feeling this same weird attraction that he was? This thing he kept trying to ignore because all it did was distract him. She was the enemy, the woman suing him. But in the dark, all he felt, smelled, touched, was Lindsay the woman.

"It might be…" She reached past him in the confined space, her hand tapping the wall. The movement brought her tighter to him, and he shifted to give her more room, but she moved at the same time, and his hands ended up on her waist. She drew in a sharp breath, and he lowered his head.

"It should be…" Her words trailed off, her breath whispering against his jaw. Hot, seductive, tempting. A flare of anger, or maybe it was desire, or maybe both, rushed through his veins. He should leave, he should get out of here, he should remember she was the one on the other side of the courtroom. "Maybe…"

"Maybe," he said, then he cursed under his breath, leaned down—

And he kissed her.

When Walker Jones's lips met hers, Lindsay stilled. Her heart raced, her breath caught in her throat, but her body went very, very still. It wasn't just the surprise—it was the feel of his lips on hers. The whisper of his mouth against hers, tender, sweet, patient.

Amazing.

It was the kind of kiss that started slow, easy, like a summer rainstorm on a wide Montana prairie. For a moment, she forgot who he was, forgot everything. She rose up into his kiss, her arm going around his neck, his going around her waist, pulling her closer. He tasted of coffee and man, and she could feel herself getting swept away.

Then she remembered his words, how he'd called this town she loved *claustrophobic*, how he'd compared it to a knitting circle. Walker Jones had no love for Rust Creek Falls, and no real concern for anything besides his bottom line.

One hot kiss in the darkness behind the gym wasn't going to change that.

She pulled away from him and as she backed into the concrete wall, the light switch poked into her back. Sure, she thought, now she found it. She flicked it on, quick. "We need to get those booths built," she said.

Yeah, that was smart—just pretend the whole thing never happened. The sooner they got back to work, the sooner they would be done, and the sooner she could put some distance between them. Walker gave her a curious look, as if he was trying to figure out what she was thinking. "Yeah, we do."

They grabbed the plywood sheets. Walker hefted two into his arms at once, while Lindsay followed behind with a single sheet. The board was heavy and awkward, which meant it required concentration to wrangle it out of the small storage room and over to the pile of wood. As soon as Lindsay dropped off the first board, she went back and got the last one. By the time she returned, Walker was busy building, and the kiss was behind them.

Or at least that's what she told herself while she handed him boards and screws and they put together the last few booths. They worked without speaking for a while.

That didn't stop her from sneaking glances at his broad back, his muscular arms, the concentration in his features as he assembled the parts. He was one hell of a kisser, and it had been a long time since she'd been kissed like that.

For a second, she'd let that kissing override the fact

that Walker was a corporate shark, with no regard for the things she loved. Even if she discounted that, and the fact that she was suing his day care chain, he was also totally devoted to his business. She'd read his bio. He'd never been engaged, and as far as she could tell, he'd only had one long-term relationship that ended a couple years ago. He'd never been involved in charity work, never done anything but work to build his empire. She'd fallen head over heels for Jeremy back in college, and in the end, he'd chosen his career over her. The bottom line triumphed over the simple life she loved.

The similarity between the two men was not lost on her. In fact, it smacked her right in the face.

Jeremy hadn't wanted to live in Rust Creek Falls. Hadn't wanted the comfortable small-town life she loved so much. He'd told her she was "wasting her talent" being a lawyer here. That had been the last straw, and the end of their relationship. She could have put the exact same words into Walker's mouth a second ago.

Ever since Jeremy, Lindsay had shied away from dating. For one, she knew pretty much every single man in Rust Creek Falls, and for another, she hadn't had the time to do anything besides study for the bar. And now she was so busy with the lawsuit, she hadn't had time to do much more than grab a drink with Lani during the week.

Walker Jones might fit the physical type of man she would be interested in, but he was the complete opposite, morally and every other way. He was driven by money, not by the values that immersed her world in Rust Creek Falls. She needed to remember that his lack of oversight, and his focus on making a profit, had nearly cost Georgina Marshall her life.

They finished the last of the booths without talking much, then stacked them against the wall. Tomorrow there'd be volunteers to paint and decorate the booths so they'd be ready for next weekend. There was still plenty to be done at the park, but building the vendor booths had been a good start.

"That was a lot of work," Lindsay said, "but I'm pretty impressed that we finished all those in one day."

Walker ran a hand over the rudimentary stalls. "I don't understand why they don't just buy some of these premade," he said. "It can't be that expensive to buy a stand like this for a festival."

She bristled. Did he really think people here had the kind of money he did? "Most of the businesses in this town don't have anything approaching a marketing budget. The owners are making do and supporting the town in the process."

"Then why have a festival at all?" He looked around the room, at the stacks of decorations, the volunteers working on hand-painted signs. "Seems to be a waste of everyone's time."

Lindsay tamped down her first response. And her second. "For your information, a festival is not a waste of anyone's time. It's not just about the booths or the sales. It's about bonding as a community."

Walker scoffed. "Bonding as a community? I hate to tell you this, sweetheart, but that's the kind of thing that only happens in novels. People are people, wherever you go, and they're not going to sit around a campfire and hold hands just because you host a harvest festival."

She parked her fists on her hips and stared up at him. "You really are that jaded, aren't you?"

"I prefer to call it realistic."

"This town bonds over more than just a harvest festival, Mr. Jones. When Jamie Stockton's wife died, this town came together to help him take care of his premature triplets. There were people there around the clock, and there still are, for no other reason than they want to help. And when your day care center started making kids sick—"

He put up his hands. "Whoa, stop right there."

She didn't stop. She kept on talking, moving toward him, angry now, at him, at herself, at that kiss. "And when your day care center started making kids sick, this town came together to support the Marshalls and the other families involved. This town isn't like some big fancy city, Mr. Jones, and that is exactly why so many people love it. And why you—" she pointed a finger at his chest "—will never fit in here, no matter how many beers you buy or booths you build."

Then she turned on her heel and headed out of the gym. As far and as fast as she could. The day when Walker Jones headed back to Tulsa couldn't come soon enough.

Chapter Five

Walker told himself he didn't care one bit what Lindsay Dalton thought of him. He didn't want her idealized small-town life, and he didn't care about this harvest festival or anything that happened in Rust Creek Falls.

For God's sake, the place sounded like something in a fairy tale. People coming together to take care of triplets, to support a family with a sick kid—that kind of thing didn't really happen. In the real world, people trampled each other to get the top spot. They looked out for number one.

He'd grown up in a driven, competitive, emotionless house. His father had only cared about what his sons achieved, and if they weren't doing anything spectacular, Walker Jones II had ignored them. Walker had thought that going to work for his father would finally win his acceptance, but if anything, it had only made his father criticize him more.

"You better do me proud," his father would say to him. "I can't have a Walker Jones who doesn't live up to the family legacy."

As if conjured up by the mere thought, Walker's phone began to buzz and his father's face appeared on the incoming call screen. Walker pushed the answer button. "It's Saturday, Dad."

"Just another day of the week," the elder Jones said. "I'm at work, and I assume you are, too."

"Of course." He didn't tell his father about building the booths, something his father would see as a waste of time. If it wasn't producing income, it wasn't worth doing.

"I'm disappointed you didn't get this frivolous lawsuit dismissed," his father said. "This should have been done and handled by now."

The implication—that Walker wasn't doing everything he could. "We go to court Tuesday. I have no doubt we will win. Their case is thin." *But their lawyer is determined.*

His father let out one of those long sighs that said he wished he'd had a son more like himself. More ruthless, more predatory. From the day Walker had started working for his father, he'd tried to live up to impossible expectations, and still failing, despite expanding Jones Holdings, Inc. to three countries and doubling its coffers in the last five years.

If Walker had turned out to be a ditch digger or trash collector, he had no doubt his father would have probably insisted he change his name. Instead, Walker had followed in his father's footsteps, doing everything he could to make his father say words he used so rarely they were like comets.

I'm proud of you.

"Handle it, Walker," his father said. "Quit letting some small-town nothing lawyer dance you around in court."

"Yes, sir." Any argument back would be pointless.

"Don't make me regret making you CEO," his father said, then he disconnected the call without a goodbye. Par for the course.

His mind wandered to Lindsay Dalton. To that kiss. To how it had distracted him from the goal.

No more. From here on out, he would deal with her in court, and nowhere else. *Handle it, Walker.*

And he would. He'd been handling things all his life, and he wasn't about to stop now because of one sentimental brunette living in some Mayberryesque town.

He pulled into the lot at Just Us Kids. The lights were still on, though he'd arrived right at the close of business on Saturday. The day care operated six days a week to allow parents who pulled weekend shifts to find child care. Business had been brisk when the day care first opened in July, but all the bad publicity about the sick kids had really hurt revenue. The bottom line was just starting to climb back into the black in the last few weeks. If he could keep news about the lawsuit from filling the front page of *The Rust Creek Falls Gazette*, then maybe this location would start turning a profit again.

Bella Stockton, the manager he'd hired in the whirlwind couple of days he'd spent here months ago, rose from her space behind the front desk when Walker entered. She was tall, probably five foot nine, and thin as a rail, as his grandmother would say. She had short blond hair and brown eyes, but always a ready smile. Even in the short interview he'd had with her, she'd impressed him as smart, organized and calm. Exactly the kind of person who should be working at a day care.

"Mr. Jones. Nice to see you again," she said.

"Call me Walker, please." He stood in the center of the lobby and looked around. The multicolored tile floor and bright crayon-colored molding were offset by sunshine-yellow walls and several child-size tables and chairs. A ceiling fan shaped like an airplane spun a lazy circle above him.

There were several new additions to the space— pictures on the wall, done by the children who attended the day care, he assumed. A row of flowers made out of handprints, a set of zoo animals drawn in crayon. There were flowers on the front desk and squishy bean bag chairs in the corner, flanked by a small bookcase stuffed with colorful books and a few baskets of toys. It looked warm and inviting, and a great introduction to the kids coming through the door, not to mention a smart way to keep children entertained while their parents were filling out paperwork or settling their bill.

"I like the changes," Walker said. He turned back to Bella. "I know my brother, so I'm assuming these things are all your doing?"

"Yes, Mr.—" She caught herself. "Walker. I just thought the lobby, particularly since it's the first thing everyone who comes through the door sees, needed to be a little more…welcoming to kids."

"I like it. Very much. Before I open the new locations, I should have you come in and offer your
opinion." He glanced around again, then nodded. He
knew it had been a good decision to hire her. "Nice
job. Very nice."

Bella blushed. "Thank you."

Walker was just about to ask where Hudson was
when the door opened and his younger brother hurried inside, along with a brisk October wind. "Hey,
sorry I'm late," Hudson said. "I had a lunch date that
almost ran into dinner." He grinned and gave Walker
a quick wink.

Walker rolled his eyes. One of these days, his bachelor brother was going to have to grow up. Hopefully
that day was today. Walker couldn't stay here in Rust
Creek Falls and babysit this location. He had a merger
with another oil refinery to oversee when he got back,
along with the upcoming day care expansion to implement. Not to mention the thousand other deals and details he managed at the corporation. If Hudson wasn't
going to step up to the plate, then Walker would un-
tangle the location entirely from his brother and open
in a new place. Let Hudson find someone else to rent
this building, and keep Walker from having to micro-
manage his younger sibling.

"Now that you're finally here, let's do a walk-
through," Walker said to Hudson. "I want to see for
myself how things are being run so I can head off
that lawyer before she tries to say we aren't keeping
on top of things."

Hudson glanced over at Bella. "You know how
things run here. Why don't you take my brother on
the big tour?"

Bella made a face. Apparently she wasn't any happier with Hudson's lack of involvement than Walker was. "I'm the manager, Hudson. Not the owner."

"Yeah, but you run the place." He gave her that grin that had undoubtedly charmed dozens of women before. "And you do a damned fine job of it, too."

Bella did not look swayed by the compliment. If anything, she seemed more annoyed by Hudson. Chances were good this wasn't the first time Hudson had tried to flirt with her. And probably one of the few times Hudson had failed to make a woman smile. Good for Bella, Walker thought. She was stronger than he'd realized. And definitely smarter.

"How about both of you show me around," Walker said. "Because apparently I'm not the only one who needs to see how this place is run."

Bella shot Walker a quick smile of agreement, then crossed to the door and flipped the sign to Closed. "Our last child left ten minutes ago, so now's a great time to do the tour." She pulled out her security badge, swiped it against the reader on the wall by the door into the center, then ushered the men through. "We keep a very tight ship here," she said. "Everyone has to have a badge, and none of the children are allowed to run around unsupervised."

"That's good." Last thing he needed now was some kid going missing. He was glad to see that Bella seemed to be on top of the security protocols and procedures he'd set in place.

As Bella ushered them down the hall, Hudson followed along behind her like a happy little puppy, watching her every move. Walker just shook his head.

Bella showed them the individual rooms for the

different age groups of children, the shelves of activities and games, the reading nooks and open coat closet spaces. "We want the rooms to feel as much like home as possible," she explained as she showed off the miniature recliners beside the bookcases. "We also have a variety of activities for all ages and levels of development. Some children prefer crafty things, some like intellectual things. One of our first steps when we take on a new child is to assess their interests and the best way that they learn. It's not school here, of course, but we do like to keep all the children, no matter their age, engaged and learning."

"That's great," Walker said. "I like that."

"We also work with the local elementary school. If one of our children is having trouble in math, for instance, we set up a quiet area for him to work one-on-one with a staff member who can help with homework or understanding concepts."

Walker nodded his approval. Hudson elbowed him. "She's smart, isn't she? Damned glad to have her here. She's always thinking up stuff like that."

Bella ignored the compliment and kept on walking. "We had a good illness prevention program in place before the outbreak of sick children, but since that day, we have increased the number of hand-sanitizing stations and been extra vigilant about cleanliness and disinfecting. We've had no problems like that since."

"That's good to hear." Walker turned to Bella. She was definitely on top of everything that happened at Just Us Kids. He made a mental note to be sure Marty planned to call her as a witness. She'd do a far better job on the stand than Hudson. "Do you think the Marshall baby got sick because of attending Just Us

Kids? Tell me the truth. I'd rather deal with that than be blindsided in court next week."

Bella glanced at Hudson. As his direct report, she no doubt felt he should be the one answering. "Uh, Hudson?"

"You know this place better than I know my own house," Hudson said. "Go ahead. Tell Walker your opinion. He won't bite."

"Yes, please," Walker echoed. "Tell me what you think happened."

"I don't think the first child contracted RSV here," Bella said, her words slow at first, then picking up speed as she realized both men were interested in her take. "We had a few kids come in here after a long weekend, coughing and sneezing. One of those midsummer colds that just seemed to take hold all over town, so it wasn't surprising to see some sniffles around here. We increased our cleaning frequency, instructed staff to wash their hands more frequently and be even more diligent about disinfecting surfaces. It was hard to tell, honestly, if it was just a cold virus or something more serious." Bella sighed. Walker could see she was still troubled about the event.

"We weren't alerted that the first child had RSV for three days. Once we knew, we sent a letter home with all the parents. If a parent brought in a sniffling child, we kept that child separated from the other kids."

To Walker, it sounded like Bella had covered all the bases. He'd read up on RSV enough to know that it did, indeed, start off as a cold, and sometimes developed into RSV in children with weakened immune systems. While the virus was spread through touching germ-filled spaces, the center had done everything within its power to reduce that likelihood. He was feeling more and more confident that the judge would agree.

"Told you," Hudson said to Walker. "She's smart. Everyone who works here thinks Bella is pretty awesome. I don't have any worries when I leave her in charge."

Hudson was singing Bella's praises, but she was not impressed. She mostly ignored Hudson, Walker noticed, and every time she did, his brother tried harder to get her attention. That was what Walker liked best about Bella—she was immune to Hudson's charms.

Which also made her perfect to be entirely in charge at Just Us Kids.

"I'm glad to hear you were on top of it, and covered all the bases," he said to her. "You've done a great job, Bella."

She blushed. "I'm just doing my job. I care about the kids."

"It shows." He glanced at his brother again. Hudson was marginally involved in the conversation—most of his attention was centered on the blonde. Clearly, Hudson had a little crush on Bella and cared more about what she thought of him than what was going on at this day care. "In fact, Bella, I want to make you full-time manager."

He named a significant pay raise, knowing she was worth that and more.

"I... I don't know what to say," Bella said. "Thank you."

"You're very welcome." Walker gave her a nod.

"You two probably want to visit," Bella said. "I'm

just going to grab my things and go home. Thank you again, Mr. Jones."

After Bella was gone, Walker and Hudson walked back through the building to the lobby. At the door, Hudson turned to Walker. "What the hell was that about?"

"What was what about?"

"You making her full-time manager. Not that I don't think Bella is doing a hell of a job, but you made it sound like I'm not even a part of this place."

"You're not. I asked you to oversee things, and protect the family interests. And instead, we've ended up with a scandal and sick kids on our hands. On your watch, I might add."

Hudson shook his head. "Yeah, oversee, not control. I never promised to be full-time, Walker. You knew I had other business interests to manage."

"The only interest I cared about was this one."

"I have been here," Hudson said. "Far more than you think."

"Oh, yeah? Then how come you looked as surprised as I was by the changes in the day care? Can you tell me the procedures for disinfection every night? Do you even know the names of everyone who works here?"

Hudson scowled. "You sound just like our father right now. Doesn't matter what I do or don't do, it's not enough for you."

The reference to their father chafed at Walker. He was nothing like the elder Jones. "I'm just running a business here, Hudson. Nothing more."

"Of course." A look that could have been disappointment, could have been hurt, filled Hudson's features. "It's not about family, it's about profits and losses."

"I'm not that callous and cold."

His brother stood there a moment, looking at the street outside the glass front door. "You know, for a minute there, when you danced at the bar and helped with the festival prep, I thought maybe you were changing," Hudson said. "Becoming more of the brother I remembered before you started working for our father. But I was wrong. You've become just like him. Cold and distant and impossible."

Walker refused to answer that. Refused to entertain the thought that Hudson's words had struck a nerve. He pushed on the door handle, then turned back. "That woman—Bella—is worth more than you think. Take care of her or you'll lose her."

Walker got in his car and pulled out of the lot. As he drove, his mind kept going back to Hudson's words. *It's not about family, it's about profits and losses.*

It bothered Walker that he and Hudson had lost that easy relationship they'd had when they were kids. Of the five Jones boys, Walker and Hudson had always gotten along the best. Maybe it was the four-year age difference, or maybe it was that Hudson's fun-loving personality had balanced Walker's serious, eldest child attitude. But as they'd gotten older and gone their separate ways, their relationship had deteriorated.

Walker had hoped—maybe foolishly—that his stay in Rust Creek Falls would be an opportunity to get back some of the relationship he had lost with Hudson. They were both adults now, and with Hudson's vested interest in the day care property, they had something more in common. But given the look of frustration on

Hudson's face earlier, Walker would put the chances of that happening at zero.

Yet another reason to leave this town as soon as possible. This lawsuit couldn't be settled fast enough for Walker's taste.

Lindsay sat in the Marshalls' living room, holding a cup of tea and feeling the ten-ton brick of their expectations hanging over her shoulders. They had been heartened by the judge's dismissal of Walker's summary judgment attempt but worried that the shortened timeline for going to court was going to impact their case. Lindsay attempted to defuse their concerns. "I think we have a strong case," she told them. "I wouldn't have taken the case if I didn't think so."

While the Marshalls seemed to relax, on the sofa across from her Dr. Jonathan Clifton put his cup on the table and leaned forward. He and his fiancée, nurse Dawn Laramie, who sat beside him, had treated Georgina during the RSV outbreak. He'd agreed to come to the Marshalls' house and talk about next week's trial, given that he would be one of the witnesses she was going to call. "It is going to be difficult to prove that the day care center was responsible, you know," he said. "This isn't a clear-cut case."

Jon had been saying that from the start. Lindsay had talked to several experts, and she knew that Walker had a point—RSV could be contracted easily, especially in children with weakened immune systems. But that didn't make Just Us Kids not responsible. They could have done more, reacted faster. In his deposition, Hudson Jones, Walker's brother and the landlord of the property, had come across as knowing little of the day-to-day details of what was going on within the doors of the center. That alone made them at least partially responsible.

If Walker or his brother had seen baby Georgina lying so frail and tiny in that hospital bed, they would have reacted just as Lindsay had—with horror that something that started out so innocuously could put a vulnerable infant on the edge of death.

"Maybe so, but the day care center should have done more to head off the further outbreak," Lindsay said. "I will argue that their laziness in disinfecting and their slow response to the crisis contributed to Georgina's illness."

Heather Marshall glanced down at her baby, asleep in her arms. Georgina was only six months old, but still so tiny, so fragile. "I just don't want any other parents to go through what we did."

"And they shouldn't. We'll make sure that Walker Jones pays for this. He can't open a day care center in this town and then just walk away from it." Lindsay could feel the fight boiling up inside her again. For a minute there, back in the gym with the booth-building project, she'd seen Walker as a man, not an adversary. She wouldn't make that mistake again.

"We have no doubts you can do this, Lindsay," Pete said. He covered his wife's hand with his own. Georgina stirred, woke up with a happy start, as she usually did, then spied Lindsay. She put out her arms in Lindsay's direction.

Heather gave her daughter an indulgent smile, then got to her feet and handed Georgina to Lindsay. Ever since the first time Lindsay had met the Marshalls' baby, the two of them had bonded. Maybe Georgina sensed all the experience Lindsay had with the Stockton triplets, or maybe she just knew Lindsay was on her side.

Lindsay rested the baby on her chest. Georgina snuggled her little face into Lindsay's neck. She fisted the soft cotton of Lindsay's shirt in one hand. The weight of the baby seemed ten times heavier because it came with all the hopes of the parents sitting across from her.

Lindsay let out a deep breath. "I worry, honestly, that I don't have the experience that you need for a case like this. I've said it before and I'll say it again—I would completely understand if you felt more comfortable with another lawyer."

Heather glanced at Pete, who gave her a little nod. She turned back to Lindsay. "We don't want another lawyer. We want you. You're a Dalton. Your family practically built this town. We know you love Rust Creek Falls and all the people here, and that means you have something a big-time lawyer from out of town wouldn't have. Heart. We know you'll do whatever it takes to win this case."

"Thank you. I appreciate your faith in me." Lindsay inhaled, and the fresh, sweet scent of baby filled her nose. Georgina's fist curled around Lindsay's finger, as if saying, *I have faith, too.* A knot twisted in her stomach. Was she really up to this challenge?

Walker Jones's attorney was more experienced, but the Marshalls were right—he didn't have the heart and soul for this town that she had. Hopefully, that would be enough.

Chapter Six

Walker had never been a big fan of holidays. Everything was shut down—banks, post office, some companies—and that meant he woke up on Monday morning expecting to get to work and realizing his day was already half-shot by the lack of availability of people he needed to talk to. Columbus Day wasn't even a real holiday, he thought, but it was real enough to leave him at loose ends.

He paced his room at Maverick Manor and debated what to do. He had a meeting with his lawyer later this afternoon, just a quick pretrial conference, but beyond that, his day was free. He'd already spent all day Sunday in his room, catching up on documents he needed to read, reviewing financial statements for his company, and cleaning out his email inbox. Even though the room was beautiful, with an expansive view of the lush green valley below and stunning mountain peaks in the distance, Walker didn't relish the idea of another day spent in here, especially when the sun was shining on a perfect fall day.

What was wrong with him? Normally he loved his job. Hardly noticed when he worked sunup to sundown. But there was something about this town—an energy—that seemed to beg him to stop working, smell the roses. Enjoy his stay.

He unfolded *The Rust Creek Falls Gazette*. There was a history of Columbus Day on the front page, then an update on the Harvest Festival preparations. He scanned over the paragraphs and noted a second volunteer event this afternoon. Something about helping with painting the signs.

Would Lindsay be there?

And why did he care? He shouldn't see her. Shouldn't spend time with her. After all, they were going to court tomorrow. Any sane man would stay far, far away from the woman suing his company.

So why was Walker in his rental car driving down the hill and back to the high school gymnasium?

He strode inside, his gaze scanning the room for Lindsay. Disappointment sank in his gut when he realized she wasn't there.

He started to turn away when he saw her coming around the corner with her sister and another man who had the same brown hair as her and Lani. The three of them were laughing at something and clearly teasing each other. The scene looked so happy, so easy.

Envy curled in his gut. He had friends, of course, and family, but he'd never had a relationship with anyone that unfurled as unfettered as a loose ribbon.

Maybe he needed to get out more. Or maybe he needed to relax a little more. Let the mountains and the valleys and the fresh air do their magic.

Or maybe just get back to work, before this whole place wrapped him any further in its lotus-eaters grip.

The happy, unstressed look disappeared from Lindsay's face when she saw Walker, and was replaced with a scowl. "What are you doing here?"

"Helping again."

She shook her head. "Stop trying to play town hero, Mr. Jones."

So they were still on *Mr. Jones*. He'd been hoping she would've rethought that formality, but their kiss only seemed to spur more animosity. Maybe she'd hated that kiss. Or maybe she hated him.

"I'm not trying to play hero. It's a holiday, so I don't have much to do for work. I wanted to keep busy, saw the mention of this volunteer day in the paper, and so here I am."

She shook her head. "It's a free country, so I can't stop you, but I also don't have to work with you. The job board is over there. Go pick anything that doesn't have my name beside it. And please, stay on your side of the gym."

Walker leaned forward and put out his hand toward the man in their group. "I'm Walker Jones, in case Lindsay here didn't already tell you. Also known as the devil incarnate."

The other man grinned. "Anderson Dalton, Lindsay's brother. If she has you on her persona non grata list, it's for a good reason. Although whatever stories she might have told you about me, I was always the innocent party."

"I have four brothers. I know what you mean. There were a lot of crimes committed by Not Me." Walker gave Lani a nod. "Nice to see you again, Lani."

She gave him a barely perceptible acknowledgment. "Mr. Jones."

Two Daltons out of three who didn't want to see him. Okay, so he'd faced better odds.

He would have walked away, but that kiss with Lindsay was still lingering in the back of his mind. Whatever she might be saying now, he was pretty damned positive he'd read interest in their embrace. If there was one thing Walker Jones didn't do, it was give up easily. So he had no intention of leaving the gym. Or, for whatever reason, letting Lindsay's negative opinion of him linger. He didn't know why it mattered to him so much, but one way or another, he was going to prove to her that he wasn't half as bad as she thought.

"Listen," Anderson said, leaning toward him and lowering his voice, "my sisters are awesome, but they're also fiercely loyal to the family, to this town, as pretty much everyone in Rust Creek Falls is. I believe in giving everyone a fair shake, especially people who want to help out and provide some free labor. So come with me and let's see if we can get you hooked up with a job to do. Preferably one I don't want to do."

Anderson and Walker laughed. He liked Lindsay's brother already, and under different circumstances, he could see the two of them playing a few holes of golf or enjoying some bourbon at a fancy bar.

Lindsay shot her brother a glare as he led Walker over to the volunteer sign-in table. Walker gave Lindsay a smile, which she ignored. He wasn't surprised, but he was more than a little disappointed. He turned back to her brother. One Dalton at a time. "So, Anderson, do you live here, too?"

"Yup. I'm a rancher, so most of my days are spent with the horses. Sometimes," he said with a quick nod toward his sisters, "they can be a lot easier to deal with than women."

Walker laughed. "You have that right. Though I don't have a lot of experience with ranches or horses. Give me a boardroom and I'm at home. But on a farm or a ranch... I wouldn't know what to do."

"It's easy. You listen to your heart." Anderson put a hand on his chest. He was taller than his sisters but had the same brown hair and blue eyes. "Your heart will tell you when a horse needs a gentler touch or the land needs some attention. Your heart will tell you whether you're running things right or running them into the ground. And your heart will always tell you if you're in the right spot—or still searching for the perfect one for you."

That could just as easily be a prescription for dealing with women, especially a beautiful, stubborn, bristly lawyer.

Walker signed his name on the page asking for people to mount the signs on posts. Anderson opted to work with him. "Sounds like you found all that here," Walker said. Anderson sounded happy, the kind of deep-rooted happiness that filled a man's soul.

A satisfied smile curved across Anderson's face. "I did. I have a fabulous wife, two great kids, and I spend my days outdoors in this beautiful Montana country. I couldn't ask for anything better."

A part of Walker envied Anderson's happiness. The

contentment in his voice. What would it be like to have that kind of…

Home. Because that was exactly what he saw shining in Anderson's eyes when he talked about his wife, his family, his town. He had found home.

Walker thought of the glass and chrome apartment he'd be returning to in a few days, smack dab in the heart of Tulsa. When he'd rented it, he'd thought it was perfect—great location, great views, great building. But never in the three years he'd lived there had he thought of it as home.

It was just this town. Being around all this…quaintness, with these neighbors straight out of a Hallmark card. This wasn't real life—or at least, not his real life. And he'd do well to remember that before he had some misplaced envy for the misty look in another guy's eyes.

The two of them were ushered over to a pile of painted boards and a stack of stakes, and they spent the next half hour attaching the boards to the stakes, then setting the signs against the wall. Other volunteers came and took the signs in bunches of six or so, to take back to the park for setup.

Lindsay and Lani had chosen to paint signs. They were on the other side of the room, and he could hear Lindsay's laughter from time to time. Everything within Walker was attuned to her, as if an invisible string tethered them together. He glanced over in her direction a thousand times, but she never even acknowledged his presence. Twice, he hit his thumb with the hammer instead of watching what he was doing.

"That's it," Anderson said a few minutes later. He brushed his hands together. "We're ahead of the sign painters, and we'll have to wait for the new signs to dry anyway before we can mount them on the stakes."

"That might take a while."

"Lucky for us, they're just now bringing in lunch." Anderson grinned. "And it's being delivered by one very beautiful woman." He waved to Walker to follow him over to several long tables set up with folding chairs and paper plates. Anderson stopped beside a redhead with blue eyes and a big smile, then gave her a kiss. "I missed you."

She laughed. "We've only been apart for a few hours."

"Long enough for me." Anderson settled a hand on the woman's waist, then gestured to Walker. "Walker, this is my wife, Marina. Marina, this is Walker Jones."

She shook his hand, then shifted back. "Wait. The same Walker Jones that Lindsay is suing?"

"She's suing my company, not me personally. I'm not such a bad guy." He gave Marina a grin, but she wasn't as easily won over as her husband. "Pleased to meet you, Mrs. Dalton."

"I have to finish getting the food set up." She turned away from Walker and placed a quick kiss on Anderson's cheek. "Save me a seat?"

"The one right next to me, of course." He smiled at her and watched her go.

The couple was clearly happy together, still in that blush of new love. Walker could see it in the way their gazes lingered on each other, the way they managed to sneak in little touches of a hand, an arm. Theresa had always been more standoffish, less flirty, and Walker had always thought that was fine. But seeing

Anderson and Marina made him wonder if perhaps he'd been missing out on something all these years.

Was Lindsay Dalton the PDA type?

Before he could question where that thought came from, and why it mattered, he shook it off. Instead, he turned to Anderson. "Your wife is beautiful," he said.

"And unfortunately not a fan of yours." Anderson chuckled. "One thing about this town, and pretty much everyone who lives here, is that loyalty runs deep."

"I'm getting that impression." He let out a long breath. He'd come to the volunteer day hoping to help out a little, connect with Lindsay and keep swaying the town's opinion of himself and his day care center. So far, he was scoring a giant zero in all three categories. "Maybe it's better if I leave."

Anderson put a hand on his shoulder. "Listen, I know there are two sides to every story. And you do strike me as a decent guy, especially since you've shown up twice to help out here. In the end, I'm Team Lindsay all the way, because she's my sister and I know she wouldn't have brought this lawsuit if she didn't think she had probable cause, but even saying that... I think you should stay and have lunch."

"Even if your sister would rather I fall off a cliff?"

Anderson chuckled. "That may be so. Either way, don't let Lindsay scare you. She's a softy at heart."

Lindsay came over just as Anderson was speaking. "Who are you calling a softy?"

"My annoying little sister, of course." Anderson gave Lindsay a faux jab to the shoulder. She feinted one back. "Anyway, I need to go help Marina set up for lunch. Why don't you and Walker get the drink station ready? There's tea and lemonade mixes in the school kitchen, and I left some big coolers down there that you can fill."

Lindsay shook her head. "I don't think—"

But Anderson had already walked off in the middle of Lindsay's sentence, leaving Walker and Lindsay to figure it out. She let out a gust of breath. "Thanks a lot, Anderson," she muttered to her brother's retreating figure.

Walker looked at Lindsay. She had her hair pulled back in a ponytail again today, which had a way of making her look more youthful and, yes, more like a softy. He liked the way the ponytail exposed the curve of her neck, the delicate loops in her ears, the slight V of her T-shirt. She might not want to be here and work with him, but he had to admit he sure didn't want her to leave. Very soon—too soon—they'd be adversaries in court again, so why not use these last few moments without the court case between them to get to know her better? What was the harm in that?

"There are going to be a bunch of hungry and thirsty people here soon," he said. "If you just show me where the kitchen is, I can fill up the coolers."

"You don't look like the kind of guy who knows how to make lemonade." She considered him, one hand on her hip.

He grinned. "You've got me there. The only cooking I've ever done consists of reheating a cup of coffee in the microwave." All his life, he'd had people who were there to make his meals, clean up after him, take care of him. Being in Rust Creek Falls was the most hands-on Walker had ever been.

And, surprisingly, he liked it. A lot.

"All right. We can work together, but—" Lindsay wagged a finger at him and spun toward the exit "—we don't need to talk while we do it."

"Oh, so we're back to that again, are we?" he said, as he followed her down the hall to the school cafeteria. The hall was empty, the lights dim. Their footsteps echoed on the polished tile floors.

"When did we ever leave that?" She pushed open the swinging metal door that led into the kitchen. Fluorescent lights flickered to life above them and bounced off an aluminum cart by the door.

Walker took one side of the metal cart, and Lindsay took the other. Two round orange drink coolers sat on a nearby counter, waiting to be filled. "Did you forget about that kiss?"

Her cheeks flushed, and she cut her gaze away. "We weren't talking while we did that, either."

That made him laugh. "No, no, we weren't. How do you do that?"

Now she lifted her blue eyes to his. They were like an ocean after a storm—tumultuous, mysterious. "Do what?"

"Turn tension into laughter." He walked around the cart, closer to her. "You have this amazing ability." He raised his hand to her face. The edge of her smile brushed against his thumb.

She stepped out of his touch. "A good trait in the opposing counsel."

"Indeed. Though I think it's too bad we are on opposite sides."

"We'd be on the same side if you acknowledged your fault," she said. This was where Lindsay felt comfortable, arguing the law. When Walker had touched her and complimented her, it had knocked her off-kilter. It was as if being outside the courtroom eliminated her ability to think straight.

"As we would be if you acknowledged the truth."

"What truth am I supposed to acknowledge?"

"That you liked that kiss back in the gym as much as I did."

His gaze held hers. She felt like she was on a witness stand, sworn to honesty. "Whether I liked it or not is immaterial. It shouldn't have happened."

He shook his head. "And there you go again, retreating into the law."

"I'm not retreating, Mr. Jones. I'm merely pointing out a fact." Okay, so maybe she was lying. But this wasn't a courtroom and she wasn't under oath and she definitely didn't want to acknowledge how many times she'd thought about that kiss.

"Just like that first day in court. You are so damned confident and defiant—"

"Stop trying to butter me up." She started to turn away, but he kept talking and she stayed where she was.

"But then I saw you playing peekaboo with the baby." He cursed under his breath. "I am not some sentimental fool, believe me. But there was something about seeing you, this strong, powerful attorney—"

"You think I'm strong and powerful?" Why couldn't she turn away? Leave the room? Stop listening?

"I think you're more than that." He shifted a degree closer. "I think you're beautiful and smart and... addictive."

"Addiction can be a bad thing." She swallowed hard, her gaze locked on his.

"It can be," he murmured.

For a moment, the air in the room stilled. Lindsay stayed where she was, breathing in, out, watching Walker. She couldn't think, couldn't speak.

Couldn't understand why she was so attracted to a man who was the opposite of everything she loved in her life.

"I don't know what it is about you," Walker said. "I know I should leave, but I just…stay."

"Me, too." The admission whispered out of her.

He shifted closer. Then he cupped her face with both his hands, leaned in and kissed her.

She curved into him as if by instinct, fitting her soft body against all his hard places, filling in the blanks. His lips danced across hers, drifting slowly at first, tasting her, learning her. Then she let out a little mew, and he opened his mouth against hers, anxious to taste her, to tango with her tongue.

In an instant, their kiss went from slow and easy to fast and wild. Hands roaming over backs, bodies pressing tight together, mouths tasting and nipping. He hoisted her onto the cart, sliding in between her legs.

The cart shifted beneath them, creaking under the added weight. Lindsay jerked to attention and pulled away from him. Her face was flushed, her chest heaving. "We can't do this. It's wrong on a thousand levels."

It was indeed. What the hell was wrong with him? Lindsay Dalton was suing him, jeopardizing the future of the day care franchise. "Not to mention, we'd be foolish to pursue anything, given that in a few days, our business will be concluded," he said.

It was a cold way to phrase whatever this was between them, but the words made it easier for him to take her second rejection.

Her gaze hardened. "You are right, Mr. Jones. Soon enough, our business will be concluded."

The echo of his own words whistled in his mind like an icy winter wind.

Once the lawsuit was over, there was no reason for Walker to stay in Rust Creek Falls. He had a competent manager for the day care and his own business to run back in Tulsa. In a few days he would be leaving—

And leaving Lindsay behind.

She hopped down off the cart and grabbed one of the coolers on the counter. "People are waiting for their drinks. We don't want to let them down. People here have already been through enough."

The hidden message in her words revealed itself clearly. When it came down to brass tacks, Lindsay Dalton's allegiance would always be to Rust Creek Falls. No matter how many kisses they shared, no matter how hot and heavy. Come tomorrow morning he was the enemy, and she was the brave knight out to slay the evil corporate dragon.

Lindsay managed to sit as far away from Walker Jones as she possibly could during lunch. But that didn't stop her from being aware of his every move, of the sound of his voice. Even twelve feet away, she could still feel his presence.

Taste his kiss.

Why did the man have to be such a good kisser? Why couldn't he have been terrible at kissing, one of those sloppy, slobbering, overeager types that she could easily resist?

Damn, he'd been so good. Too good. Making-her-crave-more-again-ASAP good.

She made small talk, laughed at jokes, held babies, talked to her brother about the ranch and the kids, but her mind remained on Walker. In the morning, they'd go back to being adversaries, and she'd go back to suing his company, for the good of the Marshalls and all the parents whose children had ended up sick.

Maybe he was just one of those charmers who tried to win the battle by making the opposition fall in love. Well, that wasn't going to happen to her. No way. No how.

No matter how well he kissed.

For the rest of the afternoon Lindsay remained on the opposite side of the gym from Walker, working on different tasks. As the projects drew to a close and she finished cleaning up, she didn't see Walker anywhere. He must have left when she wasn't looking.

She told herself she was relieved. She mostly believed it, too.

As Lindsay said her goodbyes and walked out of the gym, a misty rain began to fall. She pocketed her keys and headed toward the park, her face upturned to catch some droplets. She loved these fall days, when the air held a sharp chill, a hint of the harsh winter to come. The slight bit of rain added an air of mysticism, like she was walking into a fairy tale.

The park was quiet, empty. Leaves and small twigs crunched under Lindsay's boots, and the trees rustled against the weight of the water above her head. The mist had stopped, and the air began to clear.

She loved taking walks like this. Sometimes she'd walk the perimeter of the Dalton ranch, because the open air gave her room to think, to plan. With the trial starting tomorrow—and all the complications kissing Walker Jones had awakened—Lindsay needed this time to clear her head.

She passed the wooden booths they'd constructed earlier, waiting for the festival in a few days, then skirted the signs advertising the hay rides and hot cider. Lindsay rounded the curved path that led to the back of the Rust Creek Falls Park. Far beyond the swings and monkey bars, there was a little-used grassy area that sported one lone picnic table beneath the spreading arms of an oak tree. Mountains rose like dark sentries in the background, guarding the deep sea of trees below. Lindsay climbed onto the table, resting her feet on the seat, and leaned back, letting the approaching night wash over her.

"What a beautiful sight."

She started at the deep voice behind her and spun around. Walker Jones stood there, impossibly tall and handsome. Her heart did an instant skip beat, and her hormones rushed to center stage to stir up memories of his kiss. "Walker. You scared me."

"Sorry, I thought you heard me come up behind you." He ambled over to the front of the table and gestured to the space beside her. "Do you mind?"

Half of her wanted him to sit there, wanted a reason to brush up against him, but the other half was screaming for her to be cautious. He was her adversary, after all, not her boyfriend. Or even her friend. "We shouldn't—"

"Yeah, I know." He let out a long breath. "But it's been a long day and it's a beautiful view and I don't want to enjoy it alone."

There was something in his voice, something melancholy and lonely, that tugged at her heartstrings. Damn. Maybe Anderson was right and she was a big softy. Lindsay shifted to make room for Walker. "I love this place. I come here all the time when I get stressed out."

"Worried about tomorrow?"

"Nice try, Walker, but I won't discuss the case with you." The last thing she needed to do was tell the man she was suing that she was worried she didn't have enough of a case. That she was going to let everyone down.

That she would fail.

"Fair enough," he said. "So what should we talk about? The origins of Columbus Day? A fact I learned today, thanks to the local paper."

She laughed. Five minutes ago, she'd vowed not to let him get close again, but then he made a joke and broke the tension, and her resolve flagged. "That's big news in this town. Not a whole lot happens in Rust Creek Falls."

He shrugged. "Could be a blessing not many places have," he said. He looked around the park and shook his head, as if he couldn't quite believe what he was seeing. "This town is almost like one of those Norman Rockwell paintings. Or an episode of *Happy Days*. I feel like I'm caught in a time warp or I'm on an alien planet."

She bristled. "Come on, it's not that bad."

He looked back at her, and his eyes seemed to glimmer in the dusk. "I didn't say it was bad, necessarily... just different."

"I take it Jenks and Tulsa aren't like this?"

He scoffed. "It's not as big a city as, say, New York or Chicago, but Tulsa especially has its fair share of problems and crime. It's so busy, it seems to breathe, fast and hard, like a runner rounding a track. Everything is always moving, changing. There's nothing personal or neighborly about it. It's a city, as hard and cold as steel. But this town..." He shrugged. "Rust Creek Falls is different. And believe it or not, I can see how people would like it here."

That pleased her to no end. She loved this town, and to hear someone else say they were beginning to see its good points, too, warmed Lindsay's heart. "Rust Creek Falls has a way of getting in your blood."

He sat beside her, quiet and still, watching the sun's slow descent behind the mountains.

"Can I ask you something?" she said, then let the question out before she thought about the wisdom of getting personal with Walker. "Why open a chain of day care centers? You don't have a family of your own." She'd done her research on him in the last few days and found out he was single and childless, probably because nearly every source referred to him as *driven* and *committed* to his company. "You told me a lot about numbers and research, but you could have found any industry to expand into, rather than day cares. I don't understand why you'd want to get into a business that involved kids."

He arched a brow. "Off the record?"

"Scout's honor." She held up three fingers. "And I was a real Girl Scout for a while when I was a kid. Got my cookie badge and everything to prove it."

He chuckled. "Somehow, I can't see you as the type to take orders and build campfires."

"I'm more of a homebody than you know." She wrapped her arms around herself and drew in deep of the crisp Montana air. It was why she had returned to Rust Creek Falls after law school, why no amount of money and no job or man could tear her away from this place she loved so much. "This land, this air... it's part of my soul. I can't imagine living anywhere else. Maybe because here I can just...*be*."

"I've never known what that was like. To just *be*." The words were quiet, almost as if he didn't realize he'd admitted them.

"Not even when you were a kid?"

He shook his head, and his posture stiffened. "Like I told you, my parents were...uninvolved. We had nannies and a house big enough to fit a Boeing jet, but we didn't have a home, if that makes sense. There were so many expectations and rules and things that could break, that half the time we boys were afraid to breathe. My father was and still is a stern, exacting man, and my mother...well, she figured she did her part by giving birth to us. She got involved in her charities and left everything else up to the staff."

"I had the completely opposite childhood. We were all on the ranch, running around like a bunch of heathens, but we always felt loved." She laid her hand on his arm, for just a second. "I'm sorry you didn't grow up the same way. Every kid should have a childhood that lets them run and jump and be themselves."

He shrugged, as if it was no big deal. "It's part of why I went into the day care business. My father thought I was insane, told me I'd lose my shirt. I still might, but... I wanted to create a place where kids, regardless of what their families were like, could feel like they were at home, for a few hours a day. I researched everything, from the best color paint to the best way to find employees that would embody that spirit. For me, these centers aren't about a profit. They're about giving kids a place where they feel... loved. Like you did."

The evil, corporate-bottom-line-is-everything role she had cast Walker Jones III in didn't fit the man sitting beside her. She didn't want her heart to soften, didn't want to empathize with him, but damn it, it did— she did. There was a chance, of course, that he was lying and just telling her some sympathy-inducing story to convince her to go easy on him in court tomorrow, but Lindsay doubted it. For the first time she believed what he was telling her. This wasn't some line he was delivering, some ruse to ingratiate himself with her or the town. She had a feeling this was her first glimpse of the real Walker.

"What about a family of your own?" she asked. He was, after all, thirty-four, gorgeous, and, of course, wealthy. She figured some woman would've snatched him up long ago and he'd be married with a few kids. But then she realized how forward, how personal that question was. "Sorry, that's none of my business."

"It's okay." He let out a breath. "I met someone that I thought I would settle down with, but...let's just say she wanted more than I wanted to give. I was building the company then and working a million hours, and she wanted me to take time to enjoy life. Sleep in on Sundays and all that." He rested his elbows on his knees and looked out across the landscape. "I couldn't do that. Couldn't, in fact, imagine ever doing that…"

It seemed he was going to say more but held himself back. "Why do I get the feeling there's a *but* you didn't say?"

There was a long pause. The world was hushed, far removed from the houses and streets. It was just the two of them.

Finally he looked at her. "Very astute, counselor." He gave her a slight smile. "Maybe it's the view outside the Maverick Manor, or maybe it's seeing how all those people are coming together for one simple festival, *but*—" he emphasized the word "—this town has me thinking…*re*thinking things."

He hadn't said if meeting her had anything to do with that. And why did Lindsay care, anyway? This man was all wrong for her. Except…

This new Walker she was seeing tonight drew her closer, urged her to open up more, to get to know him better. Made her crave him in new, unexpected ways.

And that was dangerous.

Still, she couldn't stop herself.

"I had the opposite experience," she said. Had they shifted closer to each other or had she not noticed how close they were sitting? "I was engaged in law school, very briefly. I thought settling down would change my boyfriend and make him want to come back here, open up a law practice together, but his heart was set on living in New York and working in some big multi-million-dollar firm. When it became clear we wanted two entirely different lives, I broke it off."

She'd fallen for Jeremy, too, thinking he was one thing when he turned out to be another. She didn't want to make that mistake again, thinking a few minutes of sentiment from Walker Jones meant anything.

"That man was a fool," Walker said, his eyes dark in the deepening evening sky, "for letting a woman as incredible as you slip out of his life."

The words warmed the chill she'd forced into her heart a moment ago, made her think about kissing him again. She held his gaze, inhaled the spicy notes of his cologne. Damn, he even smelled good. "Are you just trying to soften me up before the trial starts?"

He grinned. "Is it working?"

"Nope. I'm not so easily swayed." She feigned affront, but in the face of his smile, it was hard to hold the pose.

He reached up, brushed a tendril of hair off her forehead and tucked the lock behind her ear. His touch lingered on her cheek, and she leaned into it. "Too bad."

"Why?" She could barely whisper the word. The desire simmering inside her was a living, breathing thing, overpowering every sane thought she'd ever had, pushing her closer to him.

"Because if you weren't Lindsay Dalton, lawyer, and I wasn't Walker Jones, owner of Just Us Kids, I think—" his gaze dropped to her lips, then back up to her eyes "—we could have been something."

"But we are those things," the sensible part of her said, even as the rest of her was telling that sensible side to shut up, "and we can't be something."

"In the morning, I'll agree with you. But right

now…" His thumb traced her bottom lip and made her breath catch. "Right now why don't we just pretend none of that exists? Just for tonight. Just for now."

Chapter Seven

Walker had no idea what the hell he was doing, getting closer to this woman, of all the women in this tiny town. He got to his feet, took Lindsay into his arms, then pressed Play on the music app on his phone. A slow-beat ballad came on, the sound a little tinny and distant coming from the small speaker. She looked up at him, her eyes wide but curious. The mist started up again, seeming to shroud them, shut them off from the rest of the town.

"I asked you to dance once before and you turned me down," he said.

"You were already dancing with another woman. Many of them, if I remember right."

He opened his arms. "Right now, you are the only one I want to dance with. So I'm asking you again. Lindsay, will you dance with me?"

She drew in a deep breath, then a smile whispered across her face. "Yes."

He put one hand on her back, clasped her palm with the other one, and pulled her into his frame. Then he began dancing with the woman who was trying to destroy his company.

But she fit so perfectly in his arms, and smelled so damned good, and already he was craving another kiss, craving her. So he danced with her, and kissed her neck, and almost came undone when she pressed into him. The song came to an end, and Walker Jones, a man who never made a move he didn't think about first, whispered five impetuous words. "Come back to my room."

"That…that changes everything," Lindsay said.

"Just being with you has changed everything." He brushed that stubborn lock of hair off her forehead again and knew, no matter what, it was going to be harder than hell to battle her in court tomorrow. Half of him wanted to wave the white flag, just to see her smile again.

"Maybe just for a drink," Lindsay said as the skies opened up and thunder began to rumble. "And only because it's raining again."

Was it? He hardly noticed. "And it's a holiday," he said.

She laughed. "A holiday is a reason to have sex?"

Once she said the two words out loud—*have sex*—his mind raced through a hundred images of them doing just that. "I think a holiday is as good a reason as any, don't you agree?"

A tease quirked a grin on her face. "I think you're giving way too much weight to Columbus Day."

"Hey, it's the whole reason we have America. I don't think the holiday gets enough weight." The rain started falling faster, so he took her hand and they dashed back through the park and over to his rental car, sliding inside just before the storm unleashed its full strength. The wipers raced to keep up with the rain as Walker pulled out of the parking lot and back toward Maverick Manor.

A rare burst of nerves rushed through his gut. Maybe because Lindsay Dalton was unlike any other woman he'd ever met. Maybe because he knew she was right and this was going to change everything, and even he wasn't sure that was a good idea. So he filled the space in the car with words.

"Did you know that Columbus Day has been celebrated since the 1700s? It wasn't made a national holiday until FDR assigned the second Monday of October as the designated day," Walker said. "Just a couple of interesting tidbits from *The Rust Creek Falls Gazette*." The words tumbled in a fast stream, like they were racing to be first out of his mouth.

She laughed. "Is this your idea of wooing a woman? Spouting historical facts?"

He glanced over at her as they pulled under the overhang in front of the hotel. "Is it working?"

"Sadly, yes." Lindsay rolled her eyes. "Either I haven't been on a date in a really long time or you have a way of making history sound sexy."

"I'm voting for sexy history." He leaned across the console, gave her a quick, hard kiss, then got out of the car and dropped his keys into the valet's palm. He came around the other side, then put out his hand to

Lindsay. "Maybe I should tell you everything I know about the life cycle of an earthworm."

Lindsay fanned her chest. "Be still, my heart. I don't think I could handle it."

Damn, he really liked this woman. No, he more than liked her. He was falling for her, for the jokes and the smiles and the way she stood toe to toe with him. She was smart and sexy and funny…and she was staying here when he went back to Tulsa. Before the thought could sour his attitude, he pushed it to the back of his mind. He'd worry about that later. Much later.

They headed inside, stopping by the bar for a bottle of wine and two glasses. "Send some strawberries and cheesecake up to my room, please," Walker said to the bartender.

"Certainly, Mr. Jones," the bartender said, keying the order into the computer. "Right away, sir."

"Strawberries and cheesecake?" Lindsay grinned as they walked away. "You really are trying to woo me."

"The cheesecake here is so good, you might not even notice me after you have the first bite." They took the elevator to the second floor. "Or you may be so overcome with gratitude that you…"

His gaze had dropped to her lips. She was standing a few inches away, and they were alone in the elevator. The warm, enclosed space seemed even tighter now, closer.

"So much gratitude that I do what?" Lindsay asked.

"That you kiss me," he said, shifting closer to her, resting his free hand on her waist, splaying his fingers along the narrow expanse above her jeans, "and don't ever want to stop."

"That would imply you are a very good kisser," she said. Her voice was low, throaty.

"And am I?"

A flush filled her cheeks, and for a moment her gaze dropped away. The shyness entranced him even more. Then she lifted her gaze back to his, all sassy and confident again. "You definitely have skills outside the boardroom, Mr. Jones."

"And you have skills outside the courtroom, Ms. Dalton." The elevator came to a stop, the doors shuddered open, but Walker took a moment to kiss her again, harder, faster this time. Desire surged between them, charging the air.

And then they were tumbling out of the elevator together, a jumble of arms and legs and wineglasses, and across the hall to his room. He fumbled with the key, twice, three times, before the door unlatched and they were inside. All the while, they kept up a heated frenzy of hungry kisses and touches.

He blindly reached for the small table inside his door, depositing the wine bottle and glasses. Then his hands were free to roam over the woman in his arms, up her back, over her curves and along her valleys. He kicked the door shut, then scooped her into his arms and crossed the small living area to enter the bedroom.

The sun had almost finished setting. A soft purple light came in through the windows, casting the room in an ethereal glow. Walker laid Lindsay on the bed, then stepped back to drink in the sight of her.

She had one arm stretched above her head, her chocolate hair in wild disarray and her shirt bunched up above her waist. She was smiling at him, her eyes dark and heavy. "What are you waiting for?"

"I want to savor this," he said. "Savor you."

That made her smile widen. She crooked her finger and beckoned him forward. "Then savor away."

He climbed onto the bed beside her. She slid into the space against his chest and kissed him. Her tongue darted into his mouth while his hand snaked under her shirt and over the curve of her breast. Even through the lace of her bra, he could feel the peak of her nipple. When he brushed one finger over the sensitive bud, she let out a gasp and arched against him.

He took a moment to tug her shirt over her head and toss it onto the floor. She was wearing a lacy white bra, and a part of him wondered if she'd done that on the off chance she would see him today. "I think I should see what else will make you gasp," he said, crooking one finger under the strap of her bra and sliding it down her arm. Her breast bulged above the cup of her bra, as if inviting him to come closer.

He dipped his head and kissed the top of the curve, then the sides, then finally brushed his lips against her nipple. She gasped again, his name escaping her lips in one long, hot whisper.

"Hmm... I think I should see what makes you gasp," she said, then slid her hand down the front of his chest, over the buckle of his jeans, then against the length of his erection. Even through the denim, he could feel the soft firmness of her touch. He wanted more. He wanted her.

"That..." He stopped; he could barely breathe, definitely couldn't think. "That will do it."

"Oh, I don't think so. I think maybe—" She paused,

flicking open the fly of his jeans, then sliding the zipper down before she slipped her hand beneath his boxers and finally—oh, holy hell—along the length of him. "This will."

He let out a gasp. "That…that works. Very well."

"I figured it might." A devilish light filled her smile.

"My turn," Walker said. He reached behind her to unfasten her bra, then slid the other strap down. He followed the path of the lace with his mouth, kissing, teasing, every inch of her neck, her chest.

She arched beneath him, her hands tangling in his hair, her breath coming faster, harder. He reached for the buckle on her jeans—

And there was a knock at the door. Three hard, fast raps.

Room service. Damn it. Why had he ordered the cheesecake?

"Give me just a second," he said to Lindsay. "And don't move." Walker started to slide off the bed when the knocking started up again.

"I know you're in there, Walker," Hudson called through the heavy wood door. "And I think it's about damned time we talked. About the day care, this lawsuit and that damned lawyer. And what the hell you think you're doing with all of it."

Lindsay bolted upright, grabbing her bra and pressing it to her chest. "Did you set this up? Catch the opposing counsel in a compromising position?"

"No, no, that's not it at all," Walker said. "Stay, please. I'll tell him to come back later."

But she was already grabbing her clothes and putting them back on. She smoothed a hand over her hair and let out a curse. "I let myself forget everything," she said. "Forget what's important. Forget why you're here. Maybe that's part of your plan—"

"That's not it, Lindsay. I got just as caught up in this as you did." Yes, getting involved with her was probably a mistake. Yes, he should have waited until after the court case, but damn it, he liked her and he wanted her, and right this second, he didn't care what happened tomorrow morning. "Lindsay, stay. Please."

But she wasn't hearing him. She was already fastened and together and at the door. "I'll see you in court tomorrow, Mr. Jones."

Mr. Jones. That was enough to tell him she was through with him.

Hudson's eyes widened when Lindsay opened the door. "What are you doing here?"

"Leaving. Which is something I should have done a while ago." She brushed past him and down the hall. She never turned back, never gave Walker a second glance.

The rain pattered softly against the windows of the kitchen, like thousands of tiny feet racing down the glass. Lindsay sat in the dark of the house where she'd grown up, eating two generous slices of apple pie. With ice cream. And whipped cream.

"Uh-oh. Must have been a bad day."

She turned at the sound of Ben Dalton's voice. The moonlight outside illuminated his tall, lean frame. "Hi, Dad. Just nervous about tomorrow." There was no way she was going to tell her father that she was trying to erase her feelings for Walker Jones with sugar and fat. Besides, it wasn't working very well.

Her chest still ached, and her brain kept reminding her that she'd been a fool for trusting that man for five seconds.

He'd set her up. Betrayed her. She dreaded court tomorrow, and Walker's lawyer telling the judge that she'd been having a relationship with Walker. She'd been so wrong about him, so wrong about everything. Walker had sweet-talked her and convinced her he was interested, then set up Hudson's appearance.

She'd never imagined Walker would stoop so low just to win a case. Or that she could be so stupid to trust the man on the other side of the courtroom.

Her father switched on the small light above the sink, casting the room in a golden glow, then took a seat on the opposite side of the table. He'd developed a little more gray hair and a few more wrinkles in recent years, but he was still the same kind, wise, patient man she'd always loved. The same man who had inspired her to go into law, to fight for the underdog, just as he had done all his life. "You're going to do fine," he said. "You're prepared, and you have a strong case. And you're on the side of right."

"I'm not so sure about that." She finished the last forkful of pie and pushed the plate to the side. "There is no one event or item to pin this RSV outbreak on. Yes, all the kids attended the same day care, but I don't have an actual definable cause."

"You have enough circumstantial evidence," her father said. "And that will weigh heavily in the judge's mind."

The closer she got to Tuesday morning, the less Lindsay believed she had what she needed to convince the judge. Maybe she shouldn't have promised the Marshalls that she could deliver justice to them for poor baby Georgina. Maybe she shouldn't have agreed to the speedier bench trial, and instead taken her chances with a jury trial. There were a thousand what-ifs that tortured Lindsay. Problem was, she couldn't change or undo any of her decisions. All she could do was try her best on Tuesday.

She looked down at the remains of her pie. All the sugar and carbs and she didn't feel any better than when she'd walked in the door. Damn that man for having a nice smile. And a sexy voice. And amazing kissing skills.

A little doubt tickled at the back of her mind. Maybe Hudson's appearance tonight had been a co-incidence, not a setup.

"There's one other thing…" Lindsay rested her palms atop one another. "I've talked to Walker Jones a few times and I'm not so sure he's the kind of guy who would run a shoddy day care."

There. She'd said it out loud. The Walker she had met seemed far from the man she'd imagined—one who protected the bottom line above the children. That was the man she'd been expecting to meet in court last week, the monster she'd created in her mind.

But the real Walker Jones III was far from that man. Either he was very, very good at acting or truly a decent man at his core. Or she was just a naive woman too blind to see the truth.

Her father arched a brow. "You've talked to the man you are suing?"

"He was volunteering for the festival prep events. We ended up working together on a couple of things—"

Ben put up his hands. "Whoa. You shouldn't be doing that. You're involved in a lawsuit against him."

"I know, I know." She sighed. "It happened by accident, really, and then I thought it would be an opportunity to see what makes him tick and maybe use that in court. But..." Her voice trailed off. She glanced at the empty pie plate. Maybe two pieces hadn't been enough to bury her regrets. She should have had three.

"You ended up liking him a little," her dad said, his voice quiet in the dim room.

She nodded, and her eyes stung a little. "Which is why I'm eating a lot of pie in the middle of the night." Not just because she'd ended up liking Walker, but because she had almost slept with him. And moreover, *wanted* to sleep with him even now, even after everything.

She needed more pie. Definitely.

Her father reached out and laid a hand on hers. "I understand. That's happened to me more than once, where I ended up liking someone I was going up against in court."

"It has?"

"Yup. Makes suing someone hard, I'll tell you. You develop a soft spot, and if there's one thing you can't show in court, it's a soft spot." Her father got to his feet, cut a slice of pie for himself, then returned to the table. It was a small sliver, because her mother would be upset if he ate too many sweets, but he'd never been able to resist her rustic apple pie. "I remember one case in particular. Remember Ronnie Hanson?"

She thought a second. "He came to you about a wrongful termination, right?"

"Yup. He worked at AJ's Bookstore for going on

fifteen years. Never late, hardly ever called in sick. One day, AJ just up and fired him. No notice, no real cause. So Ronnie came to me to ask about getting some kind of severance pay from AJ, plus the last paycheck that AJ hadn't given him. He didn't want to sue at first, but when AJ didn't answer any of my calls or letters, we got ready to go to court."

"I vaguely remember this," Lindsay said. "I was a little girl then, wasn't I?"

"Yup. Maybe five or six. Your mom, in support of Ronnie, told me she was going to stop shopping at AJ's store. Come to find out, he'd closed it already and was getting ready to leave town." Ben shook his head. "I was madder than a hornet in a beehive, thinking that AJ was trying to short Ronnie again. So I marched over to AJ's house and demanded he talk to me."

"Did he?"

Her father nodded. "We talked for four hours that day. I'd known AJ, of course, from seeing him around town, but only knew him casually. He was the kind of guy that kept to himself most days anyway. But that day, maybe he needed someone to talk to, or maybe he just wanted to explain, but he invited me in. Sat me down at his kitchen table with some coffee and some pie, just like you and I are doing right now, and started talking. By the time we were done, we'd moved on to pizza and beer—and become good friends."

Her father had always been an aboveboard, conscientious lawyer. She couldn't imagine him making the same mistake as she had and befriending the person on the other side of the courtroom. "How did that happen?"

"AJ told me why he fired Ronnie, why he hadn't sent out the last check yet. Why he was leaving town. As a father, I could understand, and that made my heart go out to him." Her father took a bite of pie, chewed it and swallowed. "Damn, your mother makes an incredible apple pie, doesn't she?"

"That's why it's won ribbons at the county fair." And was the best thing to soothe a stressed newbie lawyer.

Her father took another bite, smiled at the taste, then finished his story. "Turns out AJ had a son with another woman, one he met way before his wife. He hadn't seen much of his son in years. You know how those things go, contentious custody and all that."

Lindsay nodded. "And more often than not, it's the kids who end up suffering."

"Well, his son had been injured in a car accident, really badly. The kind of thing that would need months of rehab. Expensive rehab. This was AJ's only child—him and Beverly never did have kids of their own. So AJ did the only thing he knew to do—cashed in his business and moved to Albuquerque to be there for his son. His son healed, grew up, got married and had a son of his own. Last I heard, the two of them were planning a weeklong fishing trip and taking along AJ's grandson."

This was part of why she loved her father and wanted to be like him. He was a warm, caring and patient man who had always looked for the best in people. If he met Walker Jones, what would her father think of the driven CEO? "That's awesome."

Ben nodded. "And if I had sued AJ like I wanted to, there wouldn't have been much money left for his son's medical care. The stress alone might have given AJ a heart attack. When I saw him, he was a hair away from a nervous breakdown, because he was so worried about his son."

"So how did you settle things with Ronnie?"

"Well, once I got him calmed down—you know Ronnie, he can get as worked up as an elephant in a roomful of mice—he listened to what I had to say about AJ. I explained the situation and suggested to Ronnie that he—"

"Buy the store," Lindsay finished. She remembered this story now. She'd known Ronnie her whole life, but had forgotten how he came to be the proud owner of the local bookstore.

"Ronnie loved that place almost as much as AJ did. He got a mortgage, paid AJ what he needed, minus that last check as a compromise, then took the place over and made quite a go of it. He's still there, every single day, stocking shelves and recommending novels to customers."

"A win all around," Lindsay said.

Her father covered her hand with his own. He'd always been in her corner, always been there for her, for all the kids. "Exactly. Now if you can find one of those for this lawsuit you're in, then maybe that'll bring the Marshalls some peace and bring that smile of yours back to your face."

She tried to smile now, but the gesture fell flat. "Thanks, Dad."

He nodded, then got to his feet. "If there's one thing I've learned from being married, it's that there is no winning when it comes to the people you care about. There's only compromise. And sometimes, sweetheart, that's what you have to do in court, too. Because when it comes down to it, this isn't really about lawsuits and judgments. It's about people. Just remember that, and you'll always steer your ship along the right course."

She sat in the kitchen long after her father had gone to bed, thinking about lawsuits and courses and making the best decision for everyone. And stories that seemed one way on the surface, but were different when you looked up close for the truth. By the time the clock ticked past midnight, Lindsay didn't have any answers. Just a lot more questions—that she hoped would be answered in a court of law in the morning.

Chapter Eight

Walker parked his rental car in the courtroom lot, thirty minutes before he was due to be inside. He started scrolling through his phone, ignoring the texts from his father reminding him to step up, be a man and squash this lawsuit, when a familiar car pulled into the space beside him.

Hudson got out, then rapped on Walker's passenger side window. Walker unlocked the doors, and Hudson slid into the seat beside him. "I wanted to apologize for last night. I was pissed and drunk, and should have handled that better."

"Yeah, you should have. If you wanted to discuss something with me, you should have scheduled a time when we could talk calmly and rationally."

Hudson shook his head. "You know, I just apologized. And now you're sounding just like Dad. Schedule a time, Walker? Seriously?"

"I'm just saying—"

"No. You're just criticizing." Hudson let out a gust. "I know I'm not perfect, but neither are you. What happened to the brother I used to know?"

"I'm still your brother."

"No, Walker, you're not. You're this stranger who only cares about business, and not about people. I realize I let you down with the day care, and I am sorry for that. And I will work hard to try and make it up to you—to myself, even. But it's not like I was sitting in a bar, drinking away the days. I was building a life for myself, for my friend. A life separate from the almighty Jones Holdings."

Walker readied a retort, then stopped himself. He thought back to his words, to his actions. He had been treating Hudson more like an employee than a brother. Which was exactly the way his father treated him, only with impossible expectations. "I'm sorry. But you have to understand—"

"And there you go again, right back to justifying the way you treat me. One of these days, you're gonna look around and realize you have nothing except a cold, impersonal business." Hudson let out a long sigh. "Despite everything, you're still my brother, Walker, even if you are as uptight as a squirrel in a straight-jacket." He opened the car door. "See you inside."

Walker watched Hudson walk away, and wondered if they'd ever have a relationship again. Maybe he'd been a fool for trying to combine business with family, because it seemed all it had done was drive a wedge between the two of them. After this lawsuit was over, Walker vowed to try harder to be a brother to Hudson, not a boss.

A few minutes later, Walker sat in the same court-room, flanked once again by his lawyer, Marty. Instead of arguing a motion to get the case thrown out, they were in trial, defending Just Us Kids Day Care against Lindsay Dalton and the Marshalls. Marty was reviewing his notes, waiting for the judge's arrival.

Walker, on the other hand, was awaiting Lindsay's arrival. That alone was a sign he needed to get the hell out of this town. Since when did his interest in a woman supersede work?

Maybe since he'd met a woman who could stand toe to toe with him. A woman who could make him laugh and drive him crazy, all at the same time. A woman who intrigued and tempted him.

The door opened, and Walker pivoted to watch Lindsay stride into the courtroom. She barely flicked a glance in his direction, as if she hadn't even noticed he was there. But he noticed her. Hell, his entire body noticed her.

She was wearing a dark navy suit with a silky lavender blouse. She had her hair back in a clip, a few stray tendrils curling down the slender valley of her neck. She had a briefcase in one hand, a stack of files in thick expandable folders on her other arm and a serious, stony expression on her face.

The Marshalls followed Lindsay, and the three of them took a seat at the plaintiff's table. The grandmother came in next, with a sleepy baby Georgina in her arms. A few other people—witnesses for the plaintiffs, Walker assumed—took seats in the gallery.

"Don't worry," Marty said, following the path of Walker's gaze and clapping a hand on his shoulder. "I'm going to make sure this small-town lawyer knows better than to mess with a company like yours. She's going to run out of here with her tail between her legs. I'm going to crucify her."

Any other day, hearing those words from Marty would reassure Walker. That was what he wanted to see in his attorney—confidence and a cutthroat, take-no-prisoners approach. But today, the words churned in Walker's gut. They reminded him of Hudson's accusation that Walker was a copy of their father. "You know, she's got good intentions. Let's go a little easy on her."

Marty arched a brow. "What? Are you going soft on me now? I know I was feeling a little shaky myself on Friday, but I'm confident we can win this case, and win it well. That lawyer won't dare to come after you again."

Judge Andrews entered the courtroom. They all got to their feet and waited until the judge sat. "We have the trial scheduled today for *Marshall v. Just Us Kids Day Care*. Are counsel ready to proceed?"

"Yes, Your Honor," Lindsay said, "ready for the plaintiffs."

"The defendant is ready," Marty said.

The judge nodded toward Lindsay as Marty returned to his seat. "Very well, we'll proceed with opening statements. Ms. Dalton."

"Thank you, Your Honor." She stood and launched into her prepared comments.

Walker heard her voice but none of what she said registered on him; he was too busy looking at the woman and noticing how the suit hugged the curves he'd run his hands over last night.

"It is our position that the defendant's negligence

caused an outbreak of respiratory syncytial virus at the Just Us Kids Day Care center," she intoned. But again, Walker zoned out, his eyes drifting down to her shapely calves highlighted by the heels she wore. Only when he heard her speak his name did he drag his attention back to her eyes.

"...Mr. Jones, the owner of the center, failed to correct the dilatory hygiene practices within the center. For that reason, Just Us Kids Day Care Center should be responsible for the sizable medical bills that the Marshalls incurred as a result of the center's negligence. Thank you, Your Honor."

She nodded, then took her seat. She never once looked Walker's way or even acknowledged him. He wanted to send up a smoke signal or pass her a note or something that said *I'm sorry*.

And while he was at it, he'd apologize for his brother's interruption last night, too. Hudson had shown up at Maverick Manor at the worst possible time. Now Walker just wanted a chance to explain, to tell Lindsay it hadn't been a setup, and that he truly was interested in her.

Judge Andrews turned to Marty. "Mr. Peyton?"

Marty rose and cleared his throat. "Thank you, Your Honor. Mr. Jones was deeply saddened to hear that the Marshalls' child had been ill. But Just Us Kids Day Care has always upheld the strictest hygiene protocols and is not responsible for the transmission of a virus that even the plaintiff's attorney admits is highly contagious and easily spread. We intend to present expert testimony that RSV is common and virtually impossible to trace to one contaminant. Blaming Just Us Kids for a virus that could have come from anywhere is like blaming a single daisy for a county-wide hay fever sneezing fit."

That elicited a couple of laughs from the gallery. Lindsay shot Marty a glare.

"We intend to prove that Just Us Kids Day Care was not negligent, and therefore not responsible for this child's illness." Marty thanked the judge, then returned to his seat. He flashed Walker a smug grin.

Any other time, Walker would have been heartened by his attorney's surety, pleased by his attack. But today, winning meant hurting Lindsay, destroying the case she had worked to build. And very likely killing any chance of anything happening between them. His business would win, but his heart would lose.

Okay, so maybe that was being too dramatic. But it was ironic that once again, business was costing Walker a relationship. One that he knew was impossible, because they wanted different lives and lived in different places, and were literally on different sides, but that he still wanted to have.

Lindsay called the teary parents to the stand, one after the other. They each recounted the beginnings of their baby's illness, the scary moments in the hospital with their infant hooked up to machines to help her breathe, the fear that their child might die. Even Walker, who had told himself he was going to remain unemotional through the trial, felt his throat tighten. He could only imagine the stress and worry they'd endured.

"It was the single most terrifying week of my life," Peter Marshall said in a shaky voice. "We love Georgina more than anything in the world, and if I could have traded places with her, I would have gladly given my own breath for hers."

What would it be like to have been loved by parents like that, Walker wondered. To love a child of his own like that? Would he be a parent like the Marshalls, wholly dedicated to his child, or would he be as uninvolved and distant as his own parents had been?

He watched Lindsay questioning them and saw her eyes glisten from time to time with unshed tears. Marty muttered something about the tears being for dramatic effect, but Walker knew better. Lindsay cared—and cared deeply—about her clients, about their child, about this town.

He had no doubt what kind of mother she would be. The kind who would move heaven and earth to protect her child. A mother who would fill a home with warmth and laughter and sweet memories.

She was that kind of woman. The kind a man should marry. Plan a life with.

The thought had come out of nowhere, surprised him. He should be focused on the lawsuit—on the imminent future of Just Us Kids Day Care—and not on the future of Lindsay Dalton.

Marty got to his feet as Lindsay sat down. He glanced at his legal pad, gathering his thoughts, preparing his attack in his head. Walker had seen him do it a dozen times and knew what was coming next. Marty would circle his prey like a friendly hawk, then the second he spotted weakness, he would swoop in and exploit it until the witness crumpled.

Hell, Peter Marshall was already crumpling. He didn't need Marty's help. The father swiped at his eyes with the back of his hand. He shared a shaky smile with his wife, the two of them seeming to have a strong, silent bond.

If I could have traded places with her, I would have gladly given my own breath for hers.

Marty turned toward the witness stand. "Cute kid you have there, Mr. Marshall." Marty gave the sleeping baby in the gallery an indulgent smile. "Bet she's the apple of your eye."

Peter smiled. "You know it."

"Can't say I blame you. Kids do have a way of wrapping you around their little fingers." Marty glanced again at his pad, as if he was recalling a memory or another sweet tidbit. But Walker knew better. Marty was just feigning friendliness before circling closer. "Mr. Marshall, have you taken your baby out in public since she's been born?"

Peter let out a little laugh, as if the question was absurd. "Well, of course we have."

"To the grocery store, friends' houses, things like that?"

"Yes. But not all the time. In the beginning, she was so frail—"

"And when you took her out, did you make everyone who saw her disinfect their hands, maybe wear a face mask?" Marty asked.

Peter's brows crinkled in confusion. "Well, no, that's—"

"So if someone saw your baby, maybe held her or just chucked that adorable little girl under the chin—" Marty made the motion of doing that "—and they had maybe a touch of a cold, you would still let them get that close?"

"Well, we didn't know if everyone—"

"You didn't know if they were carrying rhinovirus germs, did you? Or maybe some kind of upper-respiratory infection?" Marty moved a few steps closer to the witness stand. "Or even maybe RSV?"

"No, but—"

"And yet you allowed those people to get close without taking proper measures to ensure there was no risk of disease?"

Lindsay shot to her feet. "Objection! Mr. Peyton is implying that my client made his daughter sick simply by living a normal life."

"Overruled. Mr. Peyton has a point about exposure, and part of your case, Ms. Dalton, is tracing the source of the infection," Judge Andrews said. He turned to the witness. "You may answer the question, Mr. Marshall."

Alarm filled Peter's face. He leaned forward, his voice earnest. "We didn't think the people who were around Georgina were carrying diseases, Mr. Peyton. We knew everyone—"

"And you knew their medical histories?"

Peter looked to Lindsay, then back at Marty. "Well, no. But that didn't mean—"

"And so you blame Mr. Jones's day care—" Marty turned to point at Walker "—for an illness that your baby could have easily contracted through your own negligence."

Now Peter saw what Marty was doing. Anger filled his eyes. "Hey! We weren't negligent. We were very careful with Georgina."

"So careful that you kept her in a little bubble?" Marty didn't wait for a response. "I didn't think so. You exposed your daughter to the world, Mr. Marshall, and that world is filled with germs. She could have gotten sick anywhere."

"But she didn't. She got sick at day care."

"How do you know that?"

"We didn't go out that week." Peter sat back against his chair, confident that he was disproving Marty's theory. But Walker knew better. Marty wouldn't have started these questions if he didn't have some kind of other knowledge. But Peter went on, oblivious to the defense counsel's plan. "And by Thursday, Georgina had a cough. By Sunday, she was in the hospital."

"So no one outside of yourself and your wife, oh, and the people at Just Us Kids, came into contact with Georgina? No one at all? Not a mailman, a pizza delivery boy, a grandmother?"

Peter's features creased. He glanced at Lindsay again, clearly hoping she'd save the day. But there was no way to undo the words Peter had already said, the admissions he'd made that he had taken his baby out among people who could be sick. Peter let out a long breath, then turned back to Marty. "I forgot that I had stopped at the neighbor's house on Monday night to pick up some cookies they had baked for me. It was my birthday the day before, and I was running home with Georgina from day care. I forgot to tell you, honey," he said to his wife. "I forgot all about it when Georgina got sick and all we thought about was making her well." He turned back to Marty. "I didn't stay long, maybe only a couple minutes."

"And did you know if those nice neighbors were a hundred percent healthy? Or whether they were…" Marty paused, like a hunter about to slay the dragon with a sword. "Sick the week before?"

"No," Peter said softly. Then a realization dawned in his eyes. He gave his wife another look of apology, and Walker could see the pain in Peter's face as he put the pieces together. "The week before, yes, one of their kids stayed home from school with a cold. But we weren't there long, and their son was all better. He was running around and laughing and—"

"You took an infant to a home that could have had lingering illness in it? Germs on the doorknob you touched, perhaps? Or maybe even a few germs on the cookies you surely ingested later? And then you handled your baby, transmitting whatever germs you picked up at the same time you picked up those cookies—"

"No, no. It was the day care center!" Peter leaned across the bench. "I know it was."

"Honestly, Mr. Marshall, you *don't* know that." Marty shook his head. "After all that, can you tell me with one hundred percent certainty that Mr. Jones's day care center was the *only* place, the *only possible* source, of your child's illness?"

Peter hung his head. "No," he mumbled. "I can't."

"No further questions." Marty spun on his heel and returned to the table with a triumphant smile on his face.

Any other day, Walker would have rejoiced with his lawyer. But today, he was left with a sick feeling in his stomach as he watched a contrite and broken Peter Marshall head back to the defendant's table to hug his wife and whisper "I'm sorry" over and over again.

Lindsay called Dr. Jonathan Clifton to the stand, followed by the doctor at the hospital, and made a strong case with each of them that the RSV was contracted at the day care center. Then Marty got his turn, and all of Lindsay's hard work was undone in a matter of minutes. She was a smart attorney, impassioned, but she was no match for Marty's experience and cutthroat instincts. He called Hudson, then Bella Stockton to the stand, along with several other workers from the day care center, and finally Walker himself, all of them making a strong and clear case that the center was clean and up to standards. Lindsay tried to negate their testimony by asking about the disinfection procedures, but in the end, Marty was a more effective questioner.

Which was why Walker had hired Marty in the first place.

But as he watched Lindsay's case fall apart, he wished he had hired a pussycat for an attorney instead of a hungry panther.

The two attorneys made their closing arguments, and the judge recessed court while he pondered his decision. Everyone got to their feet and headed out of the courtroom. Bella told Walker she had to get back to work, and Hudson offered her a ride. "Let me know what happens," he said to Walker.

"I will." He said goodbye to the two of them, then glanced across the hall, where Lindsay was talking to the Marshalls. Once again, Lindsay avoided looking at Walker. She huddled close to her clients, reassuring them in soft tones as she passed him in the aisle.

"I'm going to catch some air," Walker said to Marty. Lindsay had headed away from the courtroom as fast as possible. Her clients were standing in a corner by the soda machine, holding hands.

"Don't go far. Andrews is known to decide quickly.

He's not the kind of judge who likes to think about things for a long time. Cheer up. This is good news. You'll be out of this town before you know it."

"Yeah," Walker said, glancing again at the Marshalls. "That's good news."

He headed down the hall, away from the people milling in the tiled hall. His dress shoes echoed on the hard floor. He kept on walking until he reached a door marked Exit. A second later, he was outside, in the cool Montana air with a bright, happy sun shining on his face.

He leaned against the brick building and let out a breath. He'd never been this conflicted before, never had doubts that he was doing the right thing. It was the right decision for his company—that he knew for certain. If he lost this lawsuit, the entire future of Just Us Kids would be in jeopardy, and his father's prediction of doom for the chain would come true. Yet another black mark against his son.

But if Walker won, the Marshalls were going to be left feeling guilty for their baby's illness, and Lindsay would probably hate him for tearing apart her case.

The door beside him opened, and Lindsay stepped outside. "Oh, sorry. I didn't know you were here."

"Please, stay."

"I should get inside." She started to step back, but he reached out a hand to her.

"Please. Stay." He pushed off from the wall and stood in front of her. "I feel terrible about today."

She snorted. "Really? That's why you had your lawyer reduce my client to tears?"

"That wasn't my intent, Lindsay. I told him to go easy—"

She put up her hands. "Number one, we can't talk about this. It's an ongoing lawsuit. And number two, I don't want to talk about this with you, of all people."

"Then can we talk about something else?" He waved toward the grassy area beside the building. "It's a beautiful day. Come out and enjoy it with me. Please."

She looked over his shoulder. "I just wanted a few minutes of peace before the judge calls us back in."

"That's all I want, too. No reason we can't have those few moments together."

Her eyes met his, and he saw them glisten. "There are a hundred reasons why we can't, Walker."

"We only need one that we can." He stepped back, releasing her. "Share the wall with me, Lindsay."

She hesitated a moment longer, and his heart leaped with hope. Then she shook her head. "I can't. Because I can't be with someone who will destroy a family, all to protect a bottom line."

The door shut with a heavy, hard slam. And the sunny day suddenly seemed to dim.

Lindsay knew what the judge was going to say before he spoke. She stood in the courtroom, flanked by the Marshalls, and felt her heart sink. All that work, all that hope, wasted.

"It is the opinion of this court," Judge Andrews said, "that the plaintiffs did not prove a clear-cut source for their daughter's illness. While the illness was no doubt difficult and scary and nearly fatal, the facts do not support the claim that Mr. Jones's day care center was responsible. Therefore, judgment is for the defendant." He rapped his gavel, and it was over.

Peter and Heather turned to Lindsay. "That's it?"

Lindsay nodded. "We can appeal, but I really don't think we have much chance of overturning Judge Andrews's decision."

"I'm sorry," Peter said, taking the now awake baby from her grandmother. Georgina fussed, and Peter shifted his daughter's weight in his arms. "I really did forget about stopping at the neighbor's until just then. I was so worried about Georgina when she was sick, and when we were preparing for this lawsuit, I was just overwhelmed with work and—"

Lindsay shook her head. "It's fine, Peter. Don't blame yourself." *Blame your lawyer who didn't win today. Blame her for letting you down when you really needed someone strong in your corner.*

"But I do. We have all those bills..." He shook his head and glanced at his wife. "I'm sorry, honey."

She put a hand on his cheek, her gaze soft, her smile understanding. Heather and Peter's love for each other showed in the way they touched, talked, held together, no matter what came their way. "It's okay, Peter. Georgina is well again. We have a wonderful family, and we're just going to move forward from here."

Hearing a sound behind them, Lindsay turned and saw Walker standing there. He was the last person she wanted to see right now, and definitely the last one Peter and Heather wanted to see. "What are you doing here? Gloating over your win?"

"No. I'm here to speak to the Marshalls." He put out his hand, but neither Peter nor Heather took it. Walker let his hand drop. "I wanted to say I'm sorry for all your family has been through."

Heather scowled. "It was your fault, your day care's fault. Regardless of what the judge said."

Georgina started to cry, as if she was agreeing, too. Peter tried to soothe his daughter, but she was having none of that. Heather took the baby, but still Georgina cried. Heather blew her bangs out of her face and tried bouncing the baby and whispering soothing words in her ear.

"Regardless of how things turned out today," Walker said, "I would like to pay your medical expenses."

Lindsay's jaw dropped. "But...but you won. You are not responsible for those bills."

"I want to pay them, and would have, either way," Walker said. "Please, let me do this for you. It's the least I can do."

The Marshalls stood there, stunned and quiet. Georgina, however, was still crying and now reaching, not toward Peter or Heather or even Lindsay, but toward Walker. Her mother tried to soothe her, but Georgina only cried harder, her little hands splaying, arms straining, in Walker's direction.

He glanced at Lindsay, then back at Heather. "Is she...is she reaching for me?"

Heather was having trouble keeping her squirmy daughter in her arms. Georgina seemed determined to go over Heather's forearm and dive into Walker. "I think so. If you don't mind, just for a second, maybe it'll calm her down?"

"Uh...okay." Walker put out his hands, palms up and facing each other.

Heather laughed. "No, not like you're taking a football. Like this." She stepped forward, bending one of his arms to cradle against Georgina's back, then moving his other arm to support her weight, as she shifted the baby into the space created against Walker's chest.

"Heather, I don't think—"

But Peter's words fell on deaf ears as his wife settled their baby in Walker Jones's arms. Georgina stopped crying almost immediately and pressed her head to Walker's chest. Walker hesitated for a moment, then smiled down at the soft, sweet baby in his arms. A look of wonder filled his eyes. "I've never done this before. Are you sure I'm doing it right?"

"She's happy, isn't she?" Heather said. "That's the most important thing."

Lindsay watched Walker's features almost…melt. He was far from a natural with the baby, but within a few seconds, he was swaying gently left to right, holding Georgina against his chest like she'd always been there. Lindsay's resolve to hate Walker crumbled at the sight of the tiny, vulnerable child in the arms of the tall, strong bachelor. For a second, she could imagine him holding a baby of his own and doing all the things a dad would do, singing the songs, telling the bedtime stories, tucking the covers around the baby. Their baby.

Her mind froze. Where had that thought come from? What was wrong with her? She'd just lost the most important case of her young career to this man. How could she let the sight of him holding a baby change anything?

But it did, and she couldn't seem to find it in her to be mad at him another second. "Georgina really seems to like you," Lindsay said. "She doesn't settle down easily with other people."

"But why…" Walker's voice was soft, still tinged with surprise. "Why did she want me to hold her?"

"Our little girl is a stubborn fighter," Heather said. She clasped her husband's hand and the two of them smiled. "And she seems to have a good instinct for people. We might have walked into this courtroom determined to hate you, Mr. Jones, but then you made that generous offer and…"

"And we realized you're not some coldhearted CEO," Peter finished. "Thank you."

"You're welcome." The gratitude seemed to make Walker more uncomfortable than holding the baby. He suddenly shifted Georgina back into Heather's arms, then handed a business card to Peter. Walker cleared his throat, stiffened his spine and went back to being a tough CEO. "Fax the bills to my office and I will pay them as soon as I get back to Tulsa. Out of my personal funds, not my business."

Peter shook his head. "Mr. Jones, that's very generous, but—"

"You all went through a lot, Mr. Marshall, Mrs. Marshall." Walker's gaze included each of them, then paused and lingered on Georgina. A smile ghosted across Walker's face. "And I hope this helps your family heal and move forward."

Then he turned on his heel and left the courtroom. Leaving Lindsay surprised, confused and stunned.

Chapter Nine

Walker should have been on a plane heading back to Tulsa. His work here in Rust Creek Falls was done, the lawsuit settled. Due to yesterday's holiday, he was facing a cramped and shortened workweek, with scores of emails to answer, calls to make, meetings to schedule.

Yet he lingered.

Half of him hoped Lindsay would come back and say now that the lawsuit was over, she wanted to date him. But she had climbed in her car immediately after she left the courthouse and was gone before he had a chance to even wave goodbye.

He couldn't really blame her. He had, after all, won against her in court and was probably the last person she wanted to see right now. His victory rang hollow, though, and left Walker feeling not like he won, but that he had lost something very hard to find.

After thanking Marty, Walker got in his rental car and headed across town to Hudson's house, a ranch he was renting outside of town. He could have headed for the day care, but chances were better than good that Hudson was at home, especially with Bella in place as the full-time manager. That freed Hudson even more from his responsibilities. Walker knew his younger brother, and knew full well "responsible" wasn't on his personal résumé.

As expected, Hudson's car sat in the driveway. He parked, then strode up the walkway and to the door. His brother answered after the first knock. "Hey, Walker. I was just heading out."

"On a date?"

Hudson shook his head. "No, heading to the stables to help with the horses for a bit. When I get stressed, that just kind of re-centers me."

That surprised Walker. Maybe he'd been misjudging Hudson.

"Do you have a minute? So we can talk?"

Hudson hesitated, clearly still leery of another lecture from his brother. Then he stepped back and opened the door wider. "All right. But really, just for a minute."

Walker headed inside. For years, Walker had thought he and Hudson were polar opposites. But in the few days he'd been in Rust Creek Falls, he'd seen changes in Hudson. His brother, whom he'd always thought of as the irresponsible one, was investing in the ranch in Wyoming, in this town. Maybe they had more in common than he'd thought. A part of him wanted to stay right here and spend more time with Hudson, just two brothers hanging out. No business between them, nothing but friendly banter and maybe a couple games of basketball.

What was wrong with him? Was he losing his edge, his drive for corporate success? He held a baby for a few minutes and now he was wondering how he could have it all? He was good at his job, good at running his company. He didn't have time or room for anything else.

Even if, for a brief moment, he'd envied Peter and Heather Marshall and their close bond, as a couple, as a family. Even if when he'd held their baby, he had looked at Lindsay and wondered what it would be like if they were a couple. If that was their baby with soft blond curls and rosy cheeks.

But these were insane thoughts. He told himself he was better off focusing on work, on reality. Not on pipe dreams best reserved for others.

Back on track, he followed Hudson into the living room and sat in an oversize chocolate leather armchair. Hudson seemed antsy and glanced at the door every half second, while Walker, patient and stern, tried to get him to focus. Pretty much the way the two of them had been all their lives.

"Listen, I know you have this ranch in Wyoming you're helping, but I really need you to step up with the day care," Walker said.

His request had nothing to do with business, with the bottom line. It was purely personal. Selfish, really. Because if Hudson took the helm at Just Us Kids, Walker wouldn't have to return to Rust Creek Falls. Wouldn't have to risk running into the woman he was beginning to care for—and who clearly didn't feel the same about him.

Hudson waved away his oldest brother's words. "You hired Bella to do that."

"As a manager. But that doesn't mean you don't need to get in there, too. You should know how the business is running, make sure to oversee—"

"Is this going to be another beat-up-Hudson session? Because I have better things to do." Hudson started to get out of the chair.

"No. I'm sorry." Walker let out a breath. He needed to stop taking out his own frustrations on his younger brother. The fact that his relationship with Lindsay had fallen apart before it even began wasn't Hudson's fault. He rubbed his palm over his jaw and blew out a frustrated breath. "I'm not really here to talk about the center. I came because..." He hesitated. Could he do this? He was far better at weighing assets and liabilities than he was at sharing feelings and worries. But he had come here to do a job, and Walker never backed down from a difficult situation. He took a breath and charged ahead, looking his brother right in the eye. "Because I don't like how things stand between us."

Hudson's mouth opened. Closed. "Okay."

The single word was laced with suspicion. Walker couldn't blame him. Every conversation the two of them had had in the last few months had been confrontational. "You were right, when you told me I was treating you like Dad treats us. I don't mean to. I get so wrapped up in business that I forget about the personal."

"Hey, sometimes I need to be told what to do. And you have a lot on your shoulders, Walker. I wouldn't want to be working for Dad or in charge of his company. I only have to talk to him a few times a year. You see him every day."

Walker nodded. "And he's just as hard on me as ever. I keep trying to prove myself to him, as if that's going to change anything."

"The only one you need to prove something to is yourself. What matters is whether you are happy. Content. Fulfilled."

In the last few days, he could already see a thawing in the icy wall between himself and Hudson. Maybe there was a chance to build a relationship with his brother—if Walker stayed in town long enough. Problem was, the company he helmed was in Tulsa, a company with multiple interests in several industries throughout the world. It wasn't like he could just come here and run the day care. Jones Holdings, Inc. had an oil division, a finance division, a real estate division, and now the soon-to-be-expanded day care division.

Even if he did find a way to bring all that here, there was a woman in Rust Creek Falls who probably wished he'd crawl into a cave. Staying here and watching Lindsay pretend he didn't exist would be painful. Maybe he should leave now. Catch the next flight out. Forget this little town, and forget one resident in particular.

"So, how'd court go today?" Hudson asked.

Walker realized he hadn't told Hudson about the judge's decision. He'd been so focused on getting out of there, away from Lindsay's cold shoulder, that he hadn't even bothered to call or text his brother. "We won. The judge decided that there was no one event the Marshalls could point to as the cause for their daughter's illness, and cleared Just Us Kids of any negligence."

"That's great. So you're completely off the hook?"

"Yes, but..." Walker let out a breath. "I didn't feel right about winning. Those parents had a legitimate worry, and even if you can't blame Just Us Kids, there's nothing to say we *weren't* at fault."

"You saw how strict Bella is with the cleanliness and stuff. Chances are slim that it was the fault of the day care," Hudson said.

"Maybe so. But I decided to pay all their medical bills anyway." Walker shrugged. "Seemed like the least I could do."

And still, it didn't feel like enough. He had this sense of things being unfinished and wondered if there was something more he could do. Something that could have a bigger impact.

"You offered to pay all their bills even after you won the case?" Hudson sat back in his chair and let out a low whistle. "So, Scrooge, where did this altruistic spirit come from?"

Walker bristled. "I'm not a Scrooge."

"You're not exactly Mother Teresa, either."

Walker started to argue, then shook his head. His brother was right. For years, Walker had been focused on the bottom line, the company's net worth, the profit margin. He sought the next takeover, the next acquisition—not the next charitable outlet. But today after court he'd had an empty feeling in his chest. Giving money to the Marshalls had eased it somewhat. He couldn't help thinking that if he gave back more, it would go away totally.

"You have a point, Hudson. I just saw how much

the Marshalls loved their daughter, and thought people like that didn't deserve to be bankrupted by something like this. I have the money to help, so I did."

Hudson smiled. "You did the right thing. That kind of action will go far in a town like this."

"I didn't do it to impress the town. I did it—"

"To impress a girl?" Hudson finished, then laughed. "Hey, I can relate. I'm not above handing over my jacket on a chilly night or opening a door if it impresses a pretty girl."

"Yeah, well, it didn't work." Walker envied his younger brother's easy way with women. Maybe if Walker had a little of that charm and confidence, he could have wooed Lindsay Dalton and not left the courtroom feeling like he'd lost a limb. "That wasn't my intent in paying for the medical bills, either. Like I said, paying for the Marshalls' costs is just the right thing to do. Besides, the pretty girl isn't interested in me."

"If you're talking about that gorgeous lawyer, I think you should keep trying. The lawsuit is done, so…" Hudson put out his hands. "What's stopping you from going after her?"

"She's not interested." If he said it enough, it might stop making his chest hurt.

"She's not interested, or you're afraid to find out she doesn't like your Scroogy self?" Hudson got to his feet and crossed to the door. He put a hand on the knob. "You're fearless in business, big brother, but a scaredy-cat when it comes to women. I saw it when you were with Theresa. You always had this wall up. Like you were afraid to trust her, to really fall in love."

"And you, the poster child for bachelorhood, are the expert on this subject?"

"Hey, just because I can give the advice doesn't mean I have any intentions of taking it." Hudson grinned, the same hapless grin that had gotten him out of more than one scrape. Hudson opened the door. "Now get out of here and go track her down. Before you lose your nerve and fly back to Tulsa."

Walker got to his feet and paused by his brother. "How'd you know I was debating that very same thing?"

"We may not be close," Hudson said, laying a hand on Walker's shoulder, "but we are brothers. And in the end, I want you to be happy, Walker."

Walker met his brother's gaze, eyes so like his own it was almost like looking in a mirror. "Thanks, Hudson."

His younger brother glanced away, as if embarrassed to be caught caring. "It's nothing. Someday, I'm sure you're going to come to me and give me the same speech. Assuming I ever do something stupid like grow up."

Lindsay loved Sunday family dinners on the ranch. It was the one time when all the Daltons were together. But tonight, after her crushing loss in court hours ago, she was doubly grateful for her mother organizing a rare impromptu weeknight family meal. Maybe it would help her forget all about how she let down her clients and how Walker Jones had caught her by surprise.

Why would he go and pay for all the Marshalls' medical expenses like that? For the hundredth time, she wondered if she was wrong about him. If maybe he wasn't a bottom-line-driven corporate shark, but rather, a caring, conscientious man.

No, she knew better. She'd thought the same thing about Jeremy, then discovered he wanted a big-city life and a lot of zeros in his paycheck, not the simple home she had here. The last thing she needed was to let her heart soften toward another man who would disappoint her in the end. It had taken her too long to get over one shattered romance; she wouldn't plunge into another one doomed to the same fate.

Lindsay was in the dining room, setting the table, when her father came up and put an arm around her shoulder. "Sorry about today, kiddo."

Outside the house, a storm was raging, loud and booming. It was going to be one heck of an October thunderstorm, with drenching rains and gusty winds. The perfect night to be tucked inside the house with her family.

She paused in laying out the forks. "I really thought we had a good case."

"You knew it was going to be an uphill battle, honey. But it's okay. Losses teach us more than successes do."

Lindsay scoffed. "Remind me of that when I take on my next clients." She folded a napkin and tucked it under the silverware. "Maybe I'd be better off sticking to working on power of attorney forms and wills."

Her father gave her shoulder a gentle squeeze. "You have the right instincts, honey, and you have the heart of a lion. The legal world needs more of that. You'll win the next one."

"But I really wanted to make a difference for the

Marshalls, and all those families whose babies got sick." Instead, she'd let her clients down. Let Georgina down. Let the evil corporate giant win.

Ben turned her until she was facing him. "You did. You believed them, and supported them, and fought for them. Sometimes, that's all people need."

She sighed. "I hope so, Dad. I really do."

Her father gave her a smile, then headed into the kitchen to help her mother put the finishing touches on dinner. Lindsay finished setting the table just as Anderson and Marina and their two kids, Jake and baby Sydney, came into the house, followed by Travis, then Lani and her fiancé, Russ. There was a flurry of greetings, then the door opened again, and Paige and Sutter walked in with their son, Carter. Right on their heels came Caleb and Mallory, with their daughter, Lily. Everyone shook off the rain and talked about the storm while dispensing hugs and kisses.

The house was loud and lively, all the siblings and in-laws exchanging small talk in a beehive of conversation. It was like the old days, when everyone lived at home and every meal was a spirited adventure. Lindsay's mom, Mary, came out of the kitchen, wiping her hands on her floral apron, then hugged all her grandkids, one at a time.

"Hey, Mom, I thought I was your favorite," Anderson said.

Mary tapped her son on his chest. "You were until I had all these adorable grandkids."

He laughed. "I understand. Heck, all I talk about now are my kids. I've become one of those dads who will show off pictures of school plays and karate lessons to every hapless soul that shows even the slightest interest."

Travis scoffed. "You've become a softy, you big wuss. You won't catch me doing anything like that."

"Anderson is not a softy," Mary said. "You wait, Travis. One of these days you'll be just the same, mark my words. Children are one of life's greatest pleasures and grandkids are twice that and more." She took her husband's hand, then gave her family a misty smile. A second later, she was back to her normal self. "Okay, everyone, dinner's served."

The family piled into the dining room, with the adults crowding around the dining room table while the older kids sat at the smaller kitchen table. There were dishes passed and jokes traded, and the usual hubbub of the Dalton clan being all together. Lindsay plated her share of the roast beef dinner though she didn't seem to have much of an appetite tonight.

Before they dug in, at the other end of the table Anderson tapped his wineglass with a knife. "I'd like everyone's attention," he called out over the din. When it was quiet, he raised his glass. "I'd like to propose a toast. To my sister, a great lawyer."

Lindsay couldn't believe his words. Hadn't he heard what happened in court today? She felt her stomach clench as she looked at her oldest brother. "But I—I lost the Marshall case."

Anderson gave her a nod. "I know."

She looked around the table at her siblings and their families, all of whom were nodding as well. Then she turned to her mom and gave her a smile, now knowing why she'd called this rare weeknight meal. She took a moment to count her blessings for having the best family any woman could ask for. Then she sipped her wine and told them the woeful tale of the court case.

"In the end," she concluded, "my case just wasn't as strong as I'd hoped, and Walker had a better lawyer."

"Nobody in this town's a better lawyer than you," Anderson said as he scooped up a spoonful of mashed potatoes. "Except maybe Dad. And losing a case doesn't make you a bad lawyer. At least you went in there and tried to fight for what was right."

"I don't know about that," Lindsay said. "From what I heard at the hearing, Walker Jones had everything up to par in the day care. And there's a possibility that Georgina got sick from the neighbor's. Maybe my entire case was a waste of time."

"You're still a fabulous lawyer," Travis said, popping a whole buttermilk biscuit into his mouth. "Just do yourself a favor and win the next one."

He flashed her a patented Travis smile, and Lindsay laughed. Her brother was right. She had to put today's loss from her mind and keep on going. She'd done the best she could, and she had tried—and that's what mattered.

Suddenly hungry, she was just reaching for her fork when the doorbell rang. Travis, sitting on the corner of the table, got to his feet. "I'll get it."

Lindsay started to ask Marina about how Jake was doing in school when she heard a deep voice emanate from the foyer. A familiar deep voice. No...there was no way *he* was here. At her parents' house, during family dinner. Lindsay turned in her seat...and there he was.

Walker Jones, still wearing his suit from court, now darkened by rain, standing in the foyer.

Lani whispered, "That's Walker Jones," and the rest of the table fell silent as everyone looked from Lindsay to Walker and back again.

Lindsay shook her head and pushed back her chair. "Excuse me a second."

The only sound in the house came from the kids in the kitchen, oblivious to the tension in the dining room. Lindsay strode up to Walker, hating that just looking at him, all neat and pressed and handsome in a charcoal-gray suit, his jacket and hair wet from the rain, made her heart skip. "What are you doing here?"

"Finishing something." He took a step closer, then another, and she held her breath, expecting him to gloat over the court case or say goodbye—anything other than what he did.

He reached up and cupped her jaw, his touch tender and soft. "I don't want to leave town, Lindsay, not before we see where this thing between us is going."

For a heartbeat, she stood where she was, entranced by his touch, the look in his eyes, the words he'd spoken. Then she heard someone cough, and she remembered where she was and who she was. A Dalton, first and foremost, who remained true to her family, her town and her standards. Walker Jones didn't fit into that equation. No matter how good he looked in a suit.

"This thing, which isn't even really a thing, isn't going anywhere." She stepped back and his hand dropped away, and she told herself she wasn't disappointed.

"Pity. Because I really like you, and I think you like me, too." He drew in a breath, flicked a quick glance at her watching family, then returned his attention to her. "So I came here to officially ask you out on a date."

To ask her out? On a date? The words took a moment to sink in. Her siblings were hanging on every word, not making a secret of their eavesdropping.

"I... I..." She shook her head. Her entire family was staring at her, waiting for her to say something that involved real words. A second ago, she'd had a thousand reasons why she shouldn't be with Walker Jones, but for the life of her, she couldn't remember a single one right now. "I...can't."

Before he could reply, her mother came striding into the foyer. "Mr. Jones, come on in," Mary said, extending her hand to Walker. "We're just sitting down to dinner, but you're welcome to join us."

What was her mother doing? Didn't she know who he was? Before Lindsay could protest, Walker was handing his damp suit jacket to Travis and stepping further into the foyer.

"Thank you, ma'am. Don't mind if I do." Walker gave her mother a smile, then headed for the table. Anderson grabbed an extra chair out of the kitchen and made room for Walker across from Lindsay's seat. Travis got him a plate.

"What are you doing?" Lindsay whispered to her mother.

"That man is interested in you," Mary said. "I can see it all over his face. And I can see the same in yours."

"I'm not interested in him." Okay, so that was a lie. "Not really."

"Uh-huh. That's exactly what I said when I met your father." Understanding softened her mother's features. "That court case is all over, right? So you have no reason not to see where that thing between you two is going, like he said."

"There's nothing going on between us." Well, not exactly... There'd been a couple of kisses. And what had almost happened in his hotel room the previous night.

Okay, so maybe there was something. But it was done now. For sure.

"Nothing?" Her mother just arched a brow. "Then you won't mind if I invite an out of towner who drove all the way to the ranch in this storm to dinner?"

Walker was already talking to her family, with Anderson handing him dishes and encouraging him to fill his plate. He seemed to fit right in, as if he'd always been there. Even Lani had softened toward him. Was this some kind of alternate universe, or was her family seeing a side of Walker that Lindsay had convinced herself didn't exist?

She thought of how he'd paid the Marshalls' medical bills, even though he won the case. How he'd helped set up for the fair, even though it didn't win him any brownie points with the town. How he'd held Georgina with that look of amazement on his face. How all those things had shown her new dimensions of the man she was trying so very hard not to like.

"Go on," her mother whispered, giving Lindsay a little nudge, "and give the man half a chance."

Lindsay returned to the table and took her seat across from Walker. His gaze met hers, and a smile curved across his face. Her heart did that little flip again, and she found an answering smile lifting her own lips. "You may regret this," she said to him. "My brothers are hard on any man who comes here to see us girls."

"That's because none of the guys you dated before were worth much," Anderson said. "Hell, half of them couldn't lift a hay bale or know which end was which on a horse."

"That's your test for good boyfriend material?" Lani said. "Some kind of strong-man-in-the-barn competition?"

"I think it's a good idea," Travis said. "Weeds out the weak."

"Survival of the fittest in dating," Caleb said. "It would make a great reality show."

"Sign me up," Walker said. "There's nothing I like better than a challenge."

"Then you're dating the right girl," Anderson said, giving Walker a little nudge. "And dining with the right family."

The rest of the dinner went on that way, with the Daltons teasing Walker in between asking him questions about Tulsa and his family. She learned he'd never had a pet but he loved dogs more than cats, and, yes, he did know how to ride a horse and hoist a hay bale, thanks to the same grandfather who had taught him carpentry skills. By the time dessert was served, Lindsay half expected her mother to offer to adopt Walker.

The whole time, her heart and her brain went through a tug-of-war. Get close to Walker or push him away? Even if he was here now, he was going to leave eventually. So she hushed her heart and listened to her common sense.

Lindsay opted out of a slice of a pie and gathered

up some of the dishes. "I'm just going to get a head start on these," she said and hurried out of the room before anyone could argue with her.

She stood at the sink, washing the plates, listening to the laughter and chatter in the dining room and the play of the kids behind her. Having her family like Walker so much made resisting him ten times harder.

Give the man half a chance. Her mother's words echoed in her head. But what if she did and he turned out to be just like Jeremy? What if she fell for him and ended up disappointed and alone again? Better to just stay alone.

Lani came in, grabbed a dish towel and started drying the plates. Her sister knew, without Lindsay saying a word, why she'd left to do the dishes. "You know, he's not such a bad guy after all."

"I'm not talking about him." Lindsay circled the sponge around another plate, then rinsed it and handed it to her sister. "What does he think he's doing, showing up here?"

Okay, so maybe "not talking" about Walker needed to be redefined.

"I think he's interested in you, like he said. And you know, men have a weird way of showing that sometimes. Heck, Russ put me in jail." She grinned. "And look how that turned out."

"You and Russ are different."

"How is that? Because he's a part of this town now? Because he fit in with the family?" Lani paused for effect. "Hmm, that sort of reminds me of another man... one who is sitting in the dining room right now, purposely subjecting himself to a lot of Dalton family teasing."

Maybe Lani had a point. Russ had come from out of town and ended up settling here after he fell in love with Lani. He loved their family and had fit in like a missing piece in a puzzle. But that didn't mean Walker Jones would do the same. And why did she care if Walker stayed anyway? She wasn't interested in him.

Okay, well, maybe a teeny, tiny part of her was interested. And flattered that he'd come all the way out here, knowing her family might very well hate him because of the lawsuit, and yet he'd stayed all the same.

"Well, yeah, but..." Lindsay handed Lani the clean silverware, and the objection she had readied on her tongue fizzled away. "None of that makes Walker Jones right for me."

"Just give the man a chance," Lani whispered, echoing their mother's words. "He did, after all, come out in a terrible storm to have dinner with your family. Plus, he survived said dinner. I think that merits at least one date."

Out in the dining room, the men were getting to their feet, saying something about taking Walker out to the barn. Walker caught her gaze and held it for a long second. She could see the heat in his eyes, the interest in his features, and cursed that she felt the same way.

And that she'd just been bamboozled by her own matchmaking family.

Chapter Ten

Walker had grown up with four brothers, but never had he seen Hudson, Autry, Gideon and Jensen act like the Daltons. They were warm and affectionate, loud and teasing, and had him laughing more than he could remember doing in a long, long time. Travis, Anderson, Caleb, and even Russ and Sutter all traipsed out to the barn while the women stayed behind to clean up from dinner. Lindsay's father fell into place beside Walker. The rain had lessened, becoming soft drops instead of the heavy patter from earlier.

"You know this is all part of them making sure you're good enough for Lindsay, right?" Ben said. "This isn't a tour of the ranch—it's a test."

Walker chuckled. "If I had a sister, I'm sure I'd do the same thing."

When they stopped at the door to the barn, Lindsay's father put a hand on the wooden surface and turned to Walker. Ben's face turned serious, his gaze hard and direct. "Lindsay is my daughter, and I just want to make one thing clear. Just because you were invited to dinner and treated like one of the family doesn't mean every single one of us won't come after you if you break her heart."

Apparently the hardest grader in the Dalton family was the patriarch. Walker couldn't blame Ben for being a papa bear with his daughters. He'd do the same for any out of towner who came along, if he'd had a sister or daughter.

"I... I have no intention of doing that, sir," Walker said to Ben. To be truthful, Walker wasn't sure what his intentions were with Lindsay. All he knew was he didn't want to go back to Tulsa without at least finishing the story they had started.

"She's a strong woman and deserves the best," Ben said. "And I'm not just saying that because I'm her father."

"I understand, sir."

Ben held Walker's gaze for a long time, assessing him, measuring him. Finally, he nodded. "Okay, then." He opened the door to the barn.

As Walker followed Ben inside and back to the gentle ribbing by the other Dalton boys, Walker had the feeling he'd passed the first part of the test, but that the jury was still out on whether he would pass the entire exam in the Are You Good Enough for Lindsay Dalton class.

The problem? Walker wasn't sure where this was going to lead or whether he wanted it to lead anywhere. All he knew was that from the second he'd met Lindsay, she had intrigued and tempted him. The business side of him kept telling him to get on a plane to Tulsa, but for the first time in his life, Walker wasn't listening.

Instead, he listened to the Dalton boys riff as they headed through the stables, greeting the horses. This was a family. A real family, with all the inside jokes and shared memories. The kind of family he'd always wished he could have.

Maybe if he stayed in town longer, he could have more time with Hudson, too. Or maybe they were too old, too set in their ways, to develop the easy camaraderie the Daltons had.

He glanced through the stable window, back at the lights blazing in the house. Even through the rain, the Dalton ranch was warm, welcoming. A true home.

The one thing Walker had been looking for all his life, and he'd found it in the most unlikely of places. The very place he was going to have to leave.

The rain had finally stopped. Lindsay stepped out onto the porch and leaned against one of the posts, watching the clouds part and the first stars twinkle. The men emerged from the barn and headed back toward the house. She could pick out Walker's tall, lean frame in an instant among the sea of Dalton boys and the men who were becoming part of the Dalton clan.

She knew she should turn around and go back into the house, but something kept her rooted there as the men drew closer. Walker peeled off from the group, heading up the stairs two at a time to her.

"See you later," Anderson said, giving Walker a clap on the back. "And if you want to go riding tomorrow, just text me."

"Thanks, Anderson. I will."

The other men said good-night to Walker and headed inside, leaving her and Walker outside alone. The only sound came from fat raindrops sliding off overburdened leaves and plopping on the damp ground.

He looked handsome and relaxed, the kind of man she could curl into and feel comfortable and safe with. But Lindsay held her ground, maintained her distance. If she didn't, the temptation to be in his arms would overpower all rational thinking.

"Why did you come here?" she asked him.

"I told you. I wanted to ask you out on a date."

"Why? You're going back to Tulsa any day now, so any 'relationship' we could have—" she put air quotes around the word "—would end just as fast as it began."

He stepped closer. She caught the spicy notes of his cologne. Desire rose inside her, overriding her mind, her common sense. "Are you saying that going on a date with me would be a waste of time?"

"Well…yeah."

"I disagree. And I'd like the chance to prove it to you."

She shook her head. Why did he have to keep trying so hard? Why did she stand here, hoping he wouldn't leave? Why couldn't she just forget this man? "You don't give up easily, do you?"

"Nope. Which is a good thing in business, and in law, as I'm sure you know." He took her hand in his,

his touch warm and secure. "We'll see if that principle holds true when it comes to dating you, too."

Was he implying he wasn't going to give up on trying to win her heart? But more to the point, did she want him to keep trying? What if they ended up apart and alone anyway?

"I'm not so easily swayed." Except right now, she could be swayed into almost anything. A simple touch on her hand and she was ready to melt into his arms.

"I noticed." He gave her hand a little tug. "Come on, let's take a walk. It stopped raining and the stars are coming out."

She hesitated. She shouldn't get any more involved with this man. He didn't want the same things out of life that she did, he wasn't staying in Rust Creek Falls and she had been burned like this once before. But the feel of his hand on hers was so nice, and his smile so inviting, and damn it—she wanted him. He was like the last slice of chocolate cake, something decadent and wrong but too good to resist.

They walked along the flattened path in the grass that led past the stable and over to the corral. It was dark and quiet, and it seemed like the land beyond the ranch stretched forever into the distance. Lindsay drew in a long, deep breath. "I love the way the air smells after it rains. The world just seems…new again."

Walker drew in a breath, too, then nodded. "You know, I don't take enough time to enjoy these kinds of things. I go on maybe one vacation a year but rarely take any time off otherwise. Most days I'm working from sunrise to sunset, and the only time I spend outdoors is when I get in my car. I've spent more time in the fresh air in the few days I've been in this town than I have in the entire past year. Heck, more than I have on any vacation I've ever taken."

"I couldn't imagine a day that didn't have some time outdoors." She drew in another breath of the fresh, clean Montana air. It filled her heart, her soul, and reminded her all over again why she had chosen to live here. "It's part of why I still live on the ranch. Every acre begs you to come outside and enjoy."

He smiled at her and shook his head. "I've never known anyone like you. You're tough as nails in court, and at the same time, you're sentimental and sweet and—"

"You think I'm sweet?"

"You," he said, turning her into his arms, "are very, very sweet."

She shook her head and tried to look away from his hypnotic eyes. "You don't know me very well."

"Then give me the chance to, Lindsay."

She wanted to stay in his arms. She wanted to soak up this night, and this man, and lose herself in his touch, his kisses. But every time she thought about doing that, she circled back around to one very central fact.

Walker Jones wasn't staying.

He might enjoy a few days in Rust Creek Falls as a vacation, but he was not the type of man to stay here long term. And she had too much invested in her life here—in the people of this town—to ever leave.

"Enjoy the evening, Walker," she said as she stepped out of his embrace and pushed down the wave of disappointment in her chest. "It would be a shame to miss such a beautiful night."

Then she turned on her heel and headed back inside. As far away from Walker Jones as she could possibly get.

So, Lindsay Dalton was going to be a challenge. Walker should have expected that from the minute he'd met her. A part of him had hoped that with the lawsuit settled, they could pick up where they'd left off, but she'd made it clear that wasn't going to happen. So he'd left the ranch last night, determined to forget her.

Then he'd walked into Maverick Manor, and for the first time he'd actually taken a moment to look at the mural depicting several local families that had been painted on the wall above the reception desk. Lindsay was in it, along with her entire family. Even in the painting her blue eyes seemed to reach out to him, pull him in like a powerful magnet. And just like that he knew what he had to do. He'd canceled the airplane reservation he'd made and texted Anderson. He wasn't leaving. Not yet.

So here he was again, back on the Dalton ranch, bright and early the next day, helping Anderson with a nervous colt. Walker liked Lindsay's brother. Liked her whole family, in fact. The minute he'd arrived today, Lindsay's mother, Mary, had come out to greet him, then returned with sandwiches and icy glasses of lemonade for both him and Anderson.

He and Anderson had talked about the business of running a ranch, a common ground on which Walker felt comfortable. He was surprised to find how much of ranching corresponded to running a business in general. Just as for him, it all came down to a bottom line and always making sure there was more money coming in than going out. Anderson seemed to be doing a hell of a job running the Dalton family business and clearly loved what he did. He talked with enthusiasm about every horse, every acre and about his plans for the future. If circumstances were different and Walker lived here, he could see the two of them being friends. It made him sad to think about leaving this family behind when he returned to Tulsa.

Walker stood on the gate end of the corral, not really helping as much as playing colt control. Anderson was carrying on a one-sided conversation of soothing, melodic tones with the nervous horse. As he talked, Anderson gradually closed the gap between them. With each step Anderson took, the horse responded by prancing a bit from hoof to hoof. Anderson would pause, but he never displayed an ounce of frustration or impatience. He just kept up his steady *shush-shush* of words until the colt calmed again and they repeated the process. Approach, prance, calm. Until finally he was close enough to lay his hand on the horse's neck. The colt froze, one ear cocked to hear Anderson's murmurs. Another step, another dance of apprehension, more words, then Anderson slipped a bridle over the horse's head. He stayed there a long time, calming and soothing, until the colt was ready to be led around the corral.

As he watched the horse take tentative steps, still wary and ready to bolt at the first sign of danger, Walker realized the moment mirrored his relationship with Lindsay. He'd read definite interest in Lindsay's eyes these past few days, in her kisses, in the way she had leaned into him last night. But every time he tried to get close, she backed away again.

Anderson led the colt into a vacant stall, fed him some extra oats, then gave him one last pat before shutting the gate. The horse was still nervous but far less skittish, which Walker figured was a good sign. For the horse. Would it work that way with Lindsay?

"Let's saddle up a couple horses and take a ride," Anderson said, breaking into his thoughts.

"Sounds good." As much as Walker liked Anderson, though, he would rather be taking a ride with Lindsay. He'd called her this morning and left a voice mail inviting her along, but she'd never replied to his message. Maybe he was fighting a losing battle with her or maybe—

The door to the stables opened, ushering in a long shaft of sunlight—and Lindsay. She wasn't in her work clothes; she'd changed into jeans, a button-down chambray shirt and a pair of cowboy boots. She had her hair back in a ponytail and a well-worn Stetson seated atop her head.

His heart stopped for a second, and his breath caught in his throat while he waited for her to come inside. Right now, he was like that colt, not sure whether to move right or left or go in the opposite direction. So he stood there like an idiot and waited for her to make the first move.

"Don't tell me you're putting someone else on my favorite horse," she said to Anderson.

Someone else. Not Walker. He told himself he wasn't disappointed that she was acting like he didn't even exist.

Her brother grinned. "I wouldn't dare. I was sad-
dling her up for you."

Walker had been so distracted by Lindsay's arrival
that he hadn't even noticed that Anderson had been
readying a pair of horses, one a tall, stocky roan and
the other a strong, lean chestnut. They flanked Anderson on either side, patient and ready.

"Me? I'm not riding today." Lindsay shook her
head. "I just came by for a late lunch and then I'm
planning on sequestering myself in Dad's home office
to get some work done. I have briefs to finish tonight."

Anderson didn't listen. He led the horse up to Lindsay and put the reins in her hand, cutting off her pro-
tests. "Do me a favor. Take Walker out for a ride. Show
him the property. I've got a…sick filly to look after."

Walker decided he liked Anderson twice as much
now. Clearly, her brother was on Walker's side and trying to give him a chance to spend time with Lindsay.

Lindsay's gaze narrowed. "Which sick filly?"

"The one that needs me most." Anderson grinned,
then headed out of the stable before Lindsay could
argue. Walker and Lindsay were now alone, with just
the horses nickering softly from their stalls.

Walker led his horse up beside Lindsay's. "Does
this mean you wanted to take me up on my offer to
ride today?"

She scowled. "I came home early to work. That's
all."

Uh-huh. She could have worked just as easily in her
office, he was sure. Maybe the tough-as-nails lawyer
didn't want to admit she wanted him as much as he
wanted her. He chuckled. "Are you always this difficult to date?"

She raised her chin and stared up at him. "Are you always this stubborn?"

"Yup. Especially against someone so…challenging." He held her gaze until he saw a softening in her eyes and a flicker of a smile cross her lips. "Let's just go for a ride and forget everything else. Okay?"

For a second, he thought she was going to agree. Then the smile faded, and her gaze went to the open stable doors. It was a beautiful October day, sunny and warm enough that they wouldn't need jackets. A perfect day for being outside.

She let out a breath and shook her head. "I can't, Walker. Because in the end, it comes back to the same result. We want different things out of life. I think it's better to not get involved before either one of us has to make some hard choices."

That would mean thinking about what was going to happen when he went back to Tulsa. Eventually, he would have to return. But for now, on this sunny day, Walker didn't want to think about Oklahoma or work or anything other than this beautiful woman.

"I bet you are one hell of a chess player," he said.

Lindsay's horse shifted from hoof to hoof and let out a chuff. She ran a hand down the filly's muzzle and then patted her neck. Curiosity and a bit of a smile lit Lindsay's features. "I like chess, and have been known to play pretty competitively, yes. But what on earth does that have to do with us going for a ride?"

"Because you are always thinking ten steps ahead. Me, I just want to enjoy a beautiful day with a beautiful woman. After that, who knows?"

She shook her head. "I don't live like that, with

no plan for the future. I like to know what's coming tomorrow and the next day and the day after that."

"And I like to take risks." He stepped into one stirrup and swung his leg over the saddle, settling himself on the horse's back. Staying here in Rust Creek Falls and trying to woo a woman who kept on resisting him was definitely taking a risk. He could have taken the safe path of going back to work, but Walker was tired of that. Tired of coming home to an empty, quiet apartment. To living an empty, quiet life. He wanted more. He wanted what he'd found in that dining room last night—and he knew Lindsay was a big part of that. "Some would say opposites attract and balance each other out. So come on, Lindsay, and take a ride with me. Without any idea how the day will end, or what tomorrow will bring. Have fun. Play hooky."

He didn't want to think about tomorrow or next week or anything other than today. About filling this emptiness inside him with a woman whose smile warmed his heart.

She hesitated, her hand on the reins, her gaze on him. The horse nudged Lindsay's shoulder, clearly ready to go. "It *is* a nice day…"

"It's a *spectacular* day."

"And I do have *some* free time this afternoon…" Her mouth twitched as she considered his offer. He held his breath, waiting.

When he'd been a kid, his grandfather had taken him camping one time and taught him how to start a fire. The spark was the first part, but not the most important, his grandfather had said. Anyone could make a spark, but not everyone had the patience to coax that spark into a fire. So Walker waited, hoping the spark of interest he'd read in Lindsay's eyes would become a full-on flame.

A second later, she swung herself up into the saddle and snapped the reins. "Just because I'm going for a ride with you doesn't mean anything has changed." The sliver of a smile on her face belied her words.

"Of course not," Walker said, but as they led the horses out into the sunshine and down the grassy path to the vast acreage beyond the ranch, Walker figured a lot had changed, and he was damned glad it had.

Chapter Eleven

The giant Rust Creek Falls river spread in glistening blue glory before them. Both the horses drank from the water's edge while their tails flicked at the occasional fly. The day shone bright and happy, and as much as Lindsay wanted to say the opposite, she had to admit she was having a good time with Walker.

They'd taken an easy ride around the property while she told him stories about the horses, the Dalton family land, the history of Rust Creek Falls, its namesake waterfall and the river that wound its way through town. He took a genuine interest in what she had to say, in the stories she told about the ranches and mills that had built Rust Creek Falls into what it was today. It was intoxicating to have a man pay such close attention to her, and it made her wish the ride could go on forever. Their conversation—now that they no longer had the lawsuit between them—flowed as easily as water in a creek.

Walker unfastened a plaid blanket Anderson had strapped onto the horse's saddle earlier—probably all part of her brother's matchmaking scheme—and spread it on a grassy area beneath a wide oak tree. "Come on, have a seat. Enjoy the day."

Lindsay did as he asked, leaning back on her elbows and looking up at the dappled sun peeking behind the thick leaves. She was glad she'd agreed to go on the ride, not just because it was a glorious day, but because she was, despite her best intentions, truly enjoying her time with Walker. He was a smart, interesting man, one of the most interesting she'd ever met. He'd told her about his trips around the world, mostly business trips that took him to global destinations. He'd lived an interesting life, one far from the small town she'd inhabited most of her years. "Did you get to enjoy all those cities you went to?"

"Not nearly enough. I tend to get into work mode and weeks will go by before I spend any time outside the office. Now I see what I've been missing by working too much and taking too few vacations," he said. "Maybe I should move the corporate offices to a ranch and make outdoor lunches a mandatory thing."

For a second, she dared to hope he meant he was moving to Rust Creek Falls. But he hadn't said that, and she needed to quit looking for signs that Walker wanted the same life she did. "I try to eat lunch outside whenever the weather is good. My dad does, too. When we're in the office on the same days, we take our lunches over to the park and eat there. It's nice, because I get to pick his brain and spend time with him at the same time."

"Your family is so close," Walker said. "I used to have a friend in grade school who had a family like that. A whole bunch of brothers and sisters. It was always noisy in their house, but a good kind of noisy, if you know what I mean."

"I do." She turned over onto one elbow and looked at Walker. In jeans and a T-shirt, he looked so comfortable, relaxed. Like an entirely different man from the suited one who'd walked into the courtroom. "I was just thinking last night how nice it was to hear that noise in the house again. I've missed having all my siblings home. We're all growing up and going our separate ways."

"But at least you still get together for family dinners." Walker picked up a leaf and tossed it to the side of the blanket. "It's the kind of thing I wished I had growing up. We had plenty of money, a giant house and every single thing we could ask for, but none of us had a true home. There were no family dinners, no fights over the last piece of apple pie, nothing but this never-ending silence, it seemed. Like we were living in a bubble that no one dared break. Your family is loud and loving and awesome."

She didn't tell him that her family liked him just as much. Almost all of her siblings had texted her today to tell her that Walker was a "real catch," and that she should have him back to the house soon. "That warm space is the kind of environment you tried to create with the day care, right?"

He scoffed. "*Tried* is the operative word. Turns out I don't have the first clue how to do that. I talked to all kinds of interior designers and even a child psychiatrist before I designed the first Just Us Kids. And still, I didn't get it right. Bella was the one who added those last few touches that made it seem like home."

"I've been inside the center. It is really inviting." Even when she was suing Walker's company, she'd had to admit that the day care he'd built was far from the sterile, no-personality ones she had seen in other locations. The kids at the day care had seemed happy, too, and the staff was very hands-on and clearly enjoyed their jobs.

"Pretty much all of that was Bella Stockton's doing," Walker said. "Next time I open a location, I'm bringing her in to help with the design. She knew more about how to make it homey than all those high-priced designers I hired. And definitely more than me."

"Bella is a pretty smart woman, and really nice. Her brother is the one whose wife died after their triplets were born." From time to time, Lindsay had run into Bella when she was at Jamie's house, helping out.

"Are those the same triplets the entire town pitched in to care for?" Walker shook his head. "I swear, this town is like another planet."

"In a good way?"

"In a really good way." He rolled onto his arm and traced a line along her jaw. "There are a lot of things in this town that surprised me."

She didn't want to believe him. Didn't want to fall for his touch and his sweet words, but she couldn't stop herself. Her heart melted, and a smile found its way to her lips. "Things like what?"

"Things like...you." His thumb skimmed along her

mouth, then lingered on the bottom lip. He watched her, his eyes dark and unreadable, then slowly, ever so slowly, he closed the gap between them.

He was going to kiss her, and all those intentions she'd had not to get closer to Walker seemed very, very far away. She wanted him now—heck, she'd wanted him from that very first day—and couldn't remember a single reason why she shouldn't be with him. Maybe they were going their separate ways, with him returning to Tulsa and her staying put, but that didn't mean she couldn't enjoy one sunny afternoon with the man who made her heart race, did it?

She leaned in, meeting him halfway. When Walker's lips met hers, the simmering desire in her veins became a heated rush of want, need. His lips moved harder against hers, his tongue dipping in to play. She roamed her hands over his back, down the soft cotton of his T-shirt, over the hard denim of his jeans.

He rolled closer, his torso over hers, and reached a hand between them to cup her breast, but that wasn't enough for her. There were too many clothes, too much in the way. She hurried to unsnap the buttons on her shirt, then reached for the hem of his T-shirt and pulled it over his head. He spread the panels of her shirt, exposing her lacy bra.

He smiled down at her, then watched as he pushed back the cup and brushed a thumb over the sensitive nub. Lindsay arched against Walker, wanting more, wanting everything, wanting him.

His mouth followed the path from her jaw to her neck to her breast, while his hand slid off her shirt and undid the clasp of her bra. He paused a moment to sit back and drink in the sight of her. "You are beautiful," he said.

A flush filled her cheeks. "Thank you."

"Not just beautiful here," he said as the back of his hand skimmed along her skin, "but in your heart and mind, too. You are the most singularly interesting woman I have ever met."

She scoffed and looked away. "You've been all over the world. I'm sure you've met thousands of interesting women."

He tipped her chin until she was looking at him again. "I've never met a woman who could argue with me so effectively and at the same time have such a tender, open heart. You are fierce, Lindsay, in the way you fight, the way you love, the way you live."

Fierce. She liked that description. Liked hearing him say that. "And you are a man who challenges me, in a good way."

"Maybe because I am falling for you," he said, tracing her lips again, his blue eyes locked on hers, "and falling hard."

"Walker..." She didn't want to finish that sentence. Didn't want to tell him not to fall for her. Because tomorrow or the next day, he would be gone, and all this would be nothing more than a memory. A bittersweet memory. "When you leave, where will we be then? We live in different places, have different lives."

"Oh, Lindsay, always the lawyer, ready to argue." He grinned. "Let's not talk about any of that right now. Let's just enjoy this moment." He skipped a finger down the center of her chest. "Enjoy each other."

Her pulse raced. Maybe he was right and she needed to stop arguing, stop debating, and just...be.

It terrified her to do that. To let her heart go, to hand over the reins and trust another human being. But she looked up into Walker's eyes, and decided to take that leap.

"Yes," she said, the word coming out on a breath. "Yes." Then she rose up to kiss him.

He kissed her back, gently at first, then harder, more insistent. She matched him, move for move, and then it was a frenzy of hands on bodies, buttons undone, clothes discarded. She lay beneath Walker and ran her hands along his lean, naked body and thought he had to be one of the best-looking men she'd ever seen.

He smiled at her, a sexy, sweet smile, then started that trail of kisses again. Down her neck, along her shoulders, over her breasts, down the flat of her belly, until he reached the center of her. Her hands tangled in his hair and her breath came in gasps as he brought her to dizzying heights again and again with the masterful stroke of his tongue. When she thought she would go mad with want, he rose up again, took a second to slip on a condom, then slid into her in one long, breathtaking stroke.

She wrapped her legs around his hips and clutched at his back, whispering his name against his neck as he slid in and out of her, deeper each time, seeming to touch every nerve in her body at once. She forgot where they were, forgot what day it was, her mind a dizzying fog of Walker and pleasure.

His strokes quickened, and he leaned down to kiss her as the desire surged between them, faster, harder, until they came together in one long, hot climax. His lips lingered on hers, as if he didn't quite yet want to let go. Then, finally, he smiled at her and held her tight against him while their heartbeats slowed and the breeze cooled their skin.

Walker held Lindsay to his chest and for a long time thought the world was perfect. The birds were singing, the sun was shining, the horses were nickering softly to each other. She was warm against him, fitting perfectly into all the spaces that had been empty for too long.

But it was all only a temporary respite, and he knew that. His business was in Tulsa. He couldn't be away from it for an indefinite period of time. Hell, given how many times his cell phone had buzzed this afternoon, it sounded like everyone in the office was in some state of panic. There were undoubtedly twelve million items that all needed his immediate attention.

For the first time in his life, Walker didn't want to do any of them. He wanted to stay with this woman in this tiny little town and eat apple pie and paint signs for a festival.

He was in too deep. Had fallen too hard. Being with Lindsay Dalton would mean losing track of what mattered, of the company he was working so hard to build and expand.

His cell phone buzzed again. Walker fished it out of his pants pocket. Seven unheard voice mails. Eleven texts. And 110 emails, just from today alone. Not to mention several angry messages from his father about "abandoning his responsibilities." Walker scrolled through the messages and bit back a sigh. So much for his vacation from reality.

"I need to make some calls. We're in the middle of

this merger with another oil refinery, and the seller is talking about backing out. I need to talk to him, and calm him down."

"That's okay." Lindsay sat up and started grabbing her clothes. "We should get going anyway."

"Sorry. There's just a lot going on at work."

"No, no, it's fine." But she didn't look at him as she got dressed, and he wasn't sure what else to say. So he took the easy way out and remained silent.

The aftermath between them was filled only with the sounds of zippers zipping and snaps fastening. He folded up the blanket, tucked it back in place on the saddle, then held out a hand to help her onto her horse.

"I've got it, thanks," she said and swung her leg over the saddle, as cool and distant as she would be with a stranger.

He did the same, and a moment later, they were trotting back toward the stable. He knew he could let this silence continue and it would end here. He'd leave on the next flight, and she would just be a wonderful memory. He thought of the work he had to do, the fires he needed to put out at the office. He should be 100 percent present for all that rather than being distracted by a pretty brunette lawyer in Montana.

Yup, that was best all around.

"Let's go into town and get dinner." So much for letting it go and refocusing on work.

"Sorry, but I really do have some work to do. Maybe another day." She clicked to the horse, increasing the animal's speed. "And besides, you've got stuff you have to take care of, too."

"True. I really do need to get back to Tulsa as soon as possible." Even saying it out loud didn't make the truth any easier to accept. He saw the ranch growing nearer, and his chest tightened.

"I know you do." Her eyes were hidden by the shadows of her cowboy hat. "There's nothing else holding you here, now that the lawsuit is over."

Let it go, he told himself. *Let her go. It's for the best.*

The stable was now only thirty feet away. In seconds, they'd be back, off the horses and back to their separate lives. He'd book a flight and put this town in his rearview mirror. It was what he had wanted from the second he arrived.

Until he met Lindsay Dalton.

He tugged on one of the reins and brought his horse around in front of hers. "I don't want to go back," he said. "I don't want to leave." His phone started buzzing again, vibrating in his pocket, as if disagreeing with what he was saying.

Lindsay shook her head. "Listen, we had a nice time. A great afternoon. You don't have to say those things just because we made love."

"I'm not. I mean it, Lindsay." But work kept intruding—*buzz, buzz, buzz*. He could literally feel himself being torn in two—the half that needed to get to work against the half that wanted to go back to that river and the shady spot beneath the oak tree.

She looked away, her gaze going to someplace far, far from him. Her body was tall and stiff, no longer relaxed and easy in his arms. "We had a nice time," she said again, "but we both knew going into this that it wasn't going to last."

"What if I want more?"

"What *more*?" She swung her gaze back to his.

"Do you want to fly to Montana every other weekend? Skype a couple times a week?"

"We could do that."

"And to what end? You still run a multimillion-dollar company in Tulsa and I'm still a small-town lawyer who doesn't want to leave Rust Creek Falls. It's not like you can just up and move something like that to a place like this."

"It's not impossible," he said. But even he could hear the doubt in his voice. It wasn't impossible, but it would be a major undertaking. He'd have to hire all new staff, rebuild his local network...

Not impossible, no, but not easy, either.

"Do you really want to live in this tiny little town?" she asked, then waited for him to answer. He hesitated. "I didn't think so. And I'm not leaving here. I've already been down this road before, and so have you. You told me yourself that when it came down to choosing between your relationship and your business, you chose work."

"I was new to working for my father, trying to establish myself in his company. Then he made me CEO, and the time constraints multiplied. I couldn't do both. There simply weren't enough hours in the day to be full-time at work and full-time in a relationship."

"And what's changed now?" She shook her head. "Nothing. You're expanding, merging, buying, selling, and so on and so forth. I don't want that life, Walker. I want to stay right here in this little town where the worst thing that happens is somebody's prize pig is stolen at the county fair. I don't want the life you have, and I know that I never will."

He let out a gust. She made it sound like he'd asked

her to get married. He wasn't thinking that far in advance. He wasn't thinking past the pain of not seeing her every day. Couldn't she understand that? "I'm not saying you have to choose my world or yours right now, Lindsay. Let's just take some time together and see where we end up."

"We're eventually going to end up right where we are now. You know it, and I know it. So, we have a choice. We can end it now, after what was a—" her voice caught, the only emotion she had betrayed in the last few minutes "—wonderful afternoon, or drag this out long-distance. I vote to end it now."

He nudged his horse closer to hers. "What are you so afraid of, Lindsay?"

"I'm not afraid of anything. I'm just making the wisest decision sooner rather than later."

"It seems to me like you're running away before you get hurt." He brushed a tendril of hair behind her ear. She held his gaze but didn't betray her feelings. She was stoic, almost cold, not the warm, giving woman he'd been holding a little while ago. "You fight so hard, for this town, for the people you love, for the Marshalls, and yet when it comes to what you want, you back down as soon as it gets difficult."

"I'm being realistic, Walker. There's a difference."

"Realistic? By ending things before we see where they go?"

"Come on, Walker. You know we are different people who want different things. You may say that you want the home life that you see here, the same one you've tried to create in your day care center, but when it comes down to it, you're going right back to that cold, corporate world."

It was true. He could feel the constantly buzzing phone drawing his attention away. Half his brain was already in work mode, making lists, planning next steps. With each passing second, and each email that filled his phone, he could feel the work half gaining strength, talking him out of pursuing Lindsay any further. She was right—they lived two different lives, and no amount of Skyping was going to change that. Still, he wasn't ready to let her go. Or watch her walk away.

"You're just going to pretend today didn't happen?" he said. He already knew the answer, but needed to hear her say it. Needed that…closure. Maybe then he could move on and put Lindsay behind him.

"Wasn't that your plan, too?" She waited a beat for him to answer, and when he didn't she let out a sigh and shook her head. "That's what I thought."

She gave her horse a nudge, and a second later, they were off at a quick canter, into the stable and out of his sight.

Chapter Twelve

Lindsay did a really good job of convincing herself she was happy over the next few days.

After she brought the horse back to the stable, she'd handed the filly off to one of the workers and then beelined it out of there before Walker could catch up with her again. She'd made a huge mistake making love to him—and opening her heart.

Because despite all her best intentions, she had, indeed, begun to fall for the tall, blue-eyed CEO. He was so intriguing, with so many layers and surprises; just when she thought she knew him, he'd shown her a whole other side. Like showing up at the ranch in a rainstorm. Helping Anderson with that nervous colt. Holding Georgina after the trial.

But in the end, the reality was that he was going to leave. She'd been in that boat once before and had no intentions of falling for another man who wanted a life far from Rust Creek Falls. This was her home, her world, her family, and she never wanted to leave.

So she buried herself in her work, staying late at the office, going in early. She had no idea if Walker had gone back to Oklahoma yet. One afternoon she'd seen Hudson crossing the street and had been tempted to run over and ask him where Walker was.

But she didn't. Walker hadn't called or texted her, which meant he had done exactly what she had asked—and severed the relationship before it could go any farther.

Now, several days later, she wished he hadn't listened. Some impractical side of her dreamed of him charging in on a white horse, asking for her hand and then whisking her away toward the sunset.

She really needed to stop watching the Hallmark Channel late at night. Clearly, she'd seen one too many romance movies. To banish the sappy images, she redoubled her concentration on the papers before her, but the words just swam before her eyes.

It was Saturday, the day of the Rust Creek Falls Harvest Festival, and Lindsay was once again at her desk. She had read the same brief three times but hadn't retained a single word. Her mind was on Walker and on what he was doing right now. Was he working on the weekend, just like she was? Was he thinking of her, too?

Finally, a little after three, she pushed away from her desk and gathered up her things. Working was pointless, because she'd accomplished almost nothing in the six hours she'd been here today. She tugged on a denim jacket, locked up the office and then headed downtown. Maybe stopping at the festival would take her mind off everything.

Except the minute she saw the signs she had painted, the same signs Walker had assembled, then the row of vendor booths that she and Walker had built, everything came rushing back to her. The way he'd patiently shown her how to assemble the booths, the kiss in the back of the gym, the moment in the school cafeteria when they'd gone to make lemonade. Her heart ached, like a torn muscle, and it was all she could do to push a smile to her face and pretend everything was fine.

She greeted neighbors and friends as she made her way through the festival. She stopped at the first booth and bought a pretzel from her sister-in-law Mallory and her niece Lily. When Caleb married Mallory he'd become a great father to Mallory's adopted daughter. Lily's Chinese heritage showed in her dark hair and almond eyes, but her cowboy boots and jeans marked her as 100 percent Montana girl.

Mallory gave Lindsay a tight hug, and Lily darted over to do the same. That was one of the things Lindsay loved about this town. At every turn, there was a member of her family. And right now, she needed to be surrounded with people who mattered so she could forget the one who didn't anymore.

"Hey, girls," Lindsay said as she added a little cheese dip to her pretzel. "I didn't know you'd be working the festival."

"We're raising money for my Girl Scout troop's camping trip," Lily said. "So we made pretzels and cupcakes and cookies. Do you want some cupcakes, too, Aunt Lindsay?"

The way Lindsay was feeling right now, she was tempted to eat an entire batch of cupcakes. "Maybe later. The pretzels are delicious, though."

"Thanks." Mallory beamed. "Old family recipe."

"I'll be sure to send lots of people to your booth," Lindsay said, raising the pretzel in a goodbye wave. She made her way through the crowds, saying hello to the Traubs, and several other families.

Peter and Heather Marshall came over to Lindsay. They had baby Georgina in a stroller, all dressed up in a bright yellow coat and a pumpkin-shaped hat. She looked so adorable, and totally befitting the fall theme.

"Lindsay, we wanted to thank you again," Heather said, "for all you did."

Lindsay bent down and gave Georgina's tiny hand a little shake. The baby's mouth widened in a smile. "I wish I could have done more."

"It all turned out great in the end. True to his word, Walker paid all our medical bills, and he reached out to all the other families who had sick children and covered any expenses they had, too," Heather said. "Plus he offered each of the families a month of free day care at Just Us Kids."

She was glad to know he had kept his word. But to do the same for the other families? That went above and beyond.

"He isn't such a bad guy after all," Peter said. "Once we got to know him, he seemed genuinely nice."

Georgina started to fuss. Lindsay tried playing with the baby again, but she wasn't interested. She squirmed in her seat and started to cry.

"Got to know him?" Lindsay straightened. "You mean that day in court?"

Heather handed Georgina a teething ring of floating fish. The baby immediately started gumming the soft plastic circle. "Oh, no, he did more than that. He invited us out to dinner. He said he wanted to hear from us firsthand what we thought about the day care, to see if there were any improvements he needed to make. He went above and beyond, if you ask me."

Peter nodded agreement. "You meet some of these CEOs and they barely know what the right hand is doing with the left in their business, especially in one as big as his, where a single day care is a blip on the screen. Walker, though, is really invested in making his day care chain a success. Not just for his company but for the families who use it."

"He wants it to feel like home," Lindsay added softly. And Walker was doing that, one action at a time.

"That's exactly what he told us," Heather said. "And you know, when you have an owner who cares that much, I think that's half the battle in making a workplace feel like home."

If someone had asked her two weeks ago what she thought of Walker Jones III, "caring owner" wouldn't even have made the list. But the man she'd gotten to know did care and was committed to making things right. If she'd had any doubts about that before, they were gone now.

That only made her heart ache more. He was a good guy—an intriguing, interesting, handsome guy—but also one who lived far away and had no intentions of coming back.

Lindsay started to say goodbye to the Marshalls, then stopped. "Wait. You said Walker took you guys out to dinner. When was that?"

"Two days ago," Heather said, then laughed. "At least I think so. Georgina is getting her first tooth, so no one in our house is getting a lot of sleep lately."

Two days ago. After she'd said goodbye to him at the stable. Was it possible that Walker had stayed in town? That he hadn't gone running back to Tulsa after all?

And if that was so, why hadn't he called her? Texted? Tried to see her?

She gave the Marshalls a hug, bent down and kissed baby Georgina on the temple, then said goodbye before the emotions crowding her head could bring on tears. Maybe she had misread Walker after all. Maybe he was one of those love 'em and leave 'em guys. She was better off without him, after all.

If that was so, then why did it hurt so bad?

She stopped by Nate Crawford's booth, where he was raffling off a weekend for two at the Maverick Manor. He'd done an amazing job rebuilding the manor after he won the lottery and turned the run-down Bledsoe's Folly, as it had been nicknamed, into the gracious and beautiful hotel. With his wife, Callie, by his side, Nate looked like a happy man with a full, rich life.

"Glad to see the hotel is doing so well," Lindsay said.

"I had a flurry of bookings this week. Seems our resident millionaire recommended it to a whole bunch of his friends," Nate said. "And he's already booked a corporate retreat at the Manor for the spring."

He was still in town. Why hadn't he contacted her? "By resident millionaire you mean…"

"Walker Jones." Nate grinned. "He's been one of the best things to happen to Maverick Manor since I opened it."

What the heck was Walker doing? Taking the Marshalls out to dinner, taking care of the other families whose kids had gotten ill, increasing bookings at the Maverick Manor? She half expected someone to come up and tell her he was building a hundred-acre park next. He'd gone from town villain to town hero in the span of a week.

Refusing to spend any more time thinking about Walker, she got a cup of hot cider, bought another pretzel from her sister-in-law and tried to enjoy the festival. A local band was playing at one end of the park, filling the space with the cheery sounds of country hits. Lindsay tried to smile, tried to move to the music, but everything inside her hurt. She tossed her empty cup in the trash, then headed toward home.

The Rust Creek Falls Harvest Festival was in full swing by the time Walker arrived. He'd spent half the day in his hotel room in videoconference planning meetings with his staff. Every time he thought he'd conquered one thing on his to-do list, another twenty sprang up. Any other day, the workload might have exhausted him, driving him to hit the sheets as soon as he got home. This week, though, he'd been energized, staying up long past midnight every single night to send emails, fax signed contracts, make plans.

He had contemplated avoiding the festival entirely, because he wasn't sure his plan would be ready. It wasn't quite there yet, but maybe he could nudge things along in person. So Walker headed out of his room at the Maverick Manor and down to the park.

His phone started ringing. He pulled it out, glanced at the caller ID and decided this was a long overdue conversation. "Hello, Dad," he said when he answered.

"Are you done playing cowboy? Your responsibilities are here, Walker, not in that hick town." His father's voice was harsh.

Walker bristled. "I've worked the entire time I've been here. There are these amazing technological advances called computers that let me videoconference, sign contracts—"

"You are needed here, Walker. In person. I expect you to be back in Tulsa tomorrow."

A thousand times before, Walker had leapt to do his father's bidding, because he'd thought this action or that one would finally make his father see his son as a man to be proud of. But it seemed no matter what Walker did, his father wasn't pleased. "No."

The single word hung in the air between them. The silence went on so long, Walker was sure his father had hung up.

"I am going to pretend you didn't say that," Walker the II said. "Now, when you return—"

"I'm staying where I am. And as CEO, I'm making some changes to how Jones Holdings is run."

"You can't do that."

"I can. You put me in charge, and that means I can do what I want. I've been working with the other members of the board to implement these changes."

"You mean going behind my back to push your own agenda."

"Not at all. I'm doing what I think is best for the company," Walker paused. "And for me."

"You are going to ruin everything I worked for all my life." Disgust filled every syllable.

"No, Dad. I'm going to have the life you never had. I don't want to grow old and realize the only thing I have is a cold, empty business. I want a life. A family." Walker paused. "There's still time for you to do that, too, Dad."

"You're a fool," his father said.

"No. I *was* a fool," Walker said. "I'm not going to be one any longer." Then he hung up the phone and hurried his pace as he entered the park.

The scents of roasting hot dogs and mulled cider filled the air. A tractor with a hay-filled trailer carried loads of kids on a circuitous route outside the park. There were ring toss games and giant hopscotch patterns drawn on the grass, and vendors selling everything from handmade aprons to brightly painted Montana landscapes.

One painting caught Walker's eye as he passed the booth. A landscape of a beautiful stretch of river and the mountains that lay behind it. In the center was the unmistakable Dalton ranch. He could almost see himself and Lindsay relaxing by the river with the horses, almost hear her family sitting down to dinner.

"How much for that one?" he asked the vendor.

The woman manning the booth—the artist, he presumed, given her flowing clothes and chunky jewelry—came around to see which painting Walker was pointing at. She was tall, with wavy brown hair and kind brown eyes. "Oh, sorry, that one's not for sale."

"Everything is for sale." Walker pulled out his billfold, withdrawing a thick stack of twenties. "Name your price."

"There isn't one." The woman smiled and pushed the stack of bills away. "Not everything can be bought."

"That's the Dalton ranch in there, right?" He gestured toward the property at the base of the mountains. He could see tiny horses painted into the corral, some spring flowers on the porch. The sun was just setting in the painting, and everything had been washed with gold.

"It is. My husband's cousin's family lives there." She put out a hand. "I'm Vanessa Dalton, married to Jonah Dalton, and also the artist who painted this."

"Walker Jones," he said. "I've met your husband. Nice guy. Wait. Are you also the artist who did the mural at the Maverick Manor?"

She nodded. "Guilty as charged."

"I thought your work looked familiar." He shook hands with her, then let out a little laugh. "This really is a small town, isn't it?"

"That's what they say." Vanessa smiled again and moved away from the Dalton ranch painting. "Anyway, what about this one?" She gestured toward a painting of the town park, then at one of the mountains. "I have plenty of other landscapes of this area."

"No, this is the one I want." He looked at the painting again and felt that sense of home that he had been missing all his life. "Are you sure we can't come to an agreement?"

"I'm sorry," Vanessa said, "but it's the kind of painting that I'd like to keep in the family."

Walker could see that no amount of money was going to convince Vanessa to sell. He wasn't part of that family and had no right to ask for something that rightly belonged to the Daltons. He was always going to remain where he was—on the outside looking in. Walker said goodbye to Vanessa and made his way farther into the festival.

Maybe he should leave. What was he doing here, anyway? Working some crazy plan that very likely would explode in his face? He wandered down the pathway and thought it might be best to head back to the hotel.

Then he saw her. It was like a bolt of lightning hitting his chest. Over the last three days, Walker had told himself he was doing fine without her, but the instant he saw Lindsay, he knew that was a lie.

He wove his way through the crowds, but she was moving fast, heading for the exit. He increased his pace, then took a shortcut behind one of the booths, rounded it and ended up right in front of Lindsay. "Hey."

As opening lines went, it wasn't his best. Hell, it probably ranked right down there with the worst possible opening line he could ever say. But at the moment it was all he had.

"You're still in town."

Her words were a statement, not a question, and he could hear the hurt in her voice. Hurt that he hadn't called or texted, that he had let her go. He wanted to tell her that he had his reasons, that he'd wanted to be ready to see her, but the words refused to come. "Did you see our booths? They look great all finished."

Worst opening line followed by worst second line ever. Geesh, you'd think he was fifteen again and had no idea how to talk to women. This woman, though, was different, and he didn't want to mess up. Not any more than he already had, at least.

"Oh, yeah, I did see them. You're right. They look great." She started to brush past him. "I need to go."

He put a hand on her arm. Electricity raced through his veins. "Lindsay, wait. Please."

Her eyes glistened with unshed tears. Once again, he ached to undo the hurt from the past few days, rewind the clock, find another way. Hurting Lindsay was the last thing he wanted to do, and the only thing that had been unavoidable. They'd needed time apart—time for him to figure out what he wanted, time for her to regroup and time to pull off what he hoped was a miracle. He could only pray she would understand.

"Can we grab some hot cocoa and go talk?" he asked her.

She shook her head and pulled her arm away from his hand. "I have to go."

"Stay, Lindsay," he said, reaching out and taking her hand this time. "Stay. Just for hot cocoa."

"Walker, what is it going to accomplish? Clearly, we are done. There's no sense in prolonging the inevitable."

"Listen, I'm staying in town for a little while longer while I get a…project off the ground. We can at least be friends, right?"

She winced at the word. "Friends. Yes, of course."

Okay, it was a start. He'd gone about this all wrong from the beginning—trying to be with her when they were in the midst of a lawsuit, then getting scared immediately after they made love. It was a wonder she didn't hate him. "Friends can have hot cocoa. Right?"

"One cup of cocoa won't change anything."

He grinned. "Never underestimate the power of melted chocolate."

She gave him a wary glance. People streamed around them, heading in and out of the festival. The country band played a Randy Travis song. "One cup," Lindsay said. "That's it."

When she finally agreed, Walker felt like he'd won the lottery. "That's all I ask."

And hopefully all I need.

Lindsay should have said no. In fact, she had said no, more than once. But then Walker had beaten her at her own argument and she'd agreed. Not that her resistance was all that strong, anyway. A part of her really wanted to know why Walker was still in town. Why he hadn't called.

It was closure, she told herself. Yeah, closure. With hot cocoa.

They turned back into the festival, heading down the crowded path toward the hot chocolate booth at the back. Every few feet, Lindsay ran into someone she knew. That didn't surprise her. But what did surprise her was how many people said hello to Walker. As they walked, it began to seem more and more like he had met pretty much everyone in Rust Creek Falls. He exchanged a few words with Nick Pritchett and his wife, Cecelia, then said hello to Jonah and Vanessa Dalton. "How do you know so many residents of this town?"

"I've spent a lot of time…wandering around town, talking to people this past week," he said.

Something about Walker's answer seemed suspicious, like maybe he wasn't telling her everything. Or maybe he really had enjoyed his time in town and had made a lot of acquaintances. Word had definitely gotten around about what he had done for the families of the sick babies, because several people thanked him and welcomed him to the festival. Was that it?

Whatever had made Walker so popular, by the time they reached the hot chocolate stand, Lindsay felt like she'd gone through an entire class reunion. She was a little bit jealous that Walker had spent so much time with other people and not called or texted her all week. Why would he do that? And why was he back in her life today? Was it just a chance meeting between friends at the festival?

God, even thinking the word *friends* when it came to Walker hurt her chest. She'd wanted more, but the realistic, practical side of her knew better. No matter how many people he met here, no matter what he did, Walker was ultimately going back to Tulsa and she'd be smart to guard her heart before it got any more broken.

Natalie Crawford, who worked at her family's general store, was standing behind two huge urns filled with hot cocoa. "Hi, Lindsay. Nice to see you and…" Natalie arched a brow as she raked Walker with her eyes. "Whoever this is with you."

A weird little flare of something Lindsay refused to name as jealousy rose in her when she saw Natalie looking at Walker like he was the last bachelor on earth. Walker introduced himself, and Lindsay noticed Natalie held on just a little too long for a proper handshake.

"Two hot cocoas, please," Walker said, then glanced at Lindsay. "With whipped cream?"

"Yes." She was going to need it. That and the cupcakes Lily was selling. Maybe *all* the cupcakes.

"Extra whipped cream on both." He paid Natalie, then took the drinks from her, seeming to barely notice Natalie's attempts to flirt and smile at him. When he turned, his attention was focused squarely on Lindsay. That sent a little thrill through her and cracked the wall around her heart letting in hope. Maybe he did want more.

"M'lady," he said, executing a little bow as he gave her the cup. "Be careful. It's hot."

"Which is probably where it derived the name *hot* cocoa." She grinned at him, then took a sip. The drink was perfect, with just the right amount of whipped cream on top.

Walker and Lindsay ambled over to the playground. The festival ended just a few feet before the swings and slides, and this part of the park was deserted but still filled with the scents and sounds of the festival. She glanced over at him from time to time, wondering why a man who had shown her zero interest in the last few days was suddenly so attached. And did she dare to read something into this?

She took a seat on one of the swings and toed back and forth. Walker leaned against the frame, watching her, an amused smile playing on his lips.

"So, do you want to tell me the truth now about why so many people know you?"

He chuckled. "Why, counselor, that sounds like you're taking a deposition."

"It just seems awfully curious to me that a man who's only been in this town for little more than a week knows pretty much every single resident."

"That's a bit of an exaggeration, but yes, I've met quite a few people here over the last few days." Walker took a sip and looked out over the busy, cheery festival they'd just left. "And you're right. Rust Creek Falls is a really nice town."

She sipped at her hot cocoa and let the swing drift. The chains let out soft squeaks. "And why are you meeting so many people?"

"Well, that," he said as he bent down before her, catching the chain in one hand and bringing her to a halt right up against him, "is something I can't tell you until tomorrow."

His eyes were dark and mysterious. Tempting. She could see the slight shadow of stubble on his chin, catch the faint spicy notes of his cologne. Again today his tailored suit was gone, replaced by well-worn jeans, a thick button-down cotton shirt and a pair of boots. If she didn't know better, she'd swear Walker was born and bred in this town. "What's so special about tomorrow?"

"You'll have to meet me tomorrow morning at the corner of Commercial and South Buckskin Road, at nine. Then I can show you what I've been working on."

Her gaze narrowed. That location wasn't near the day care, so it couldn't be an expansion of the building. "What you've been working on? What do you mean?"

He put his cup on the ground, then grabbed the second chain, keeping her against his chest, so close she could kiss him without moving. "Almost from the second I let you go that day, I regretted it. But you were right—what I wanted and what you wanted were two different things. I thought I could find a way to convince you to move to Tulsa—"

She was already shaking her head. They'd circled right back to the same place. She should have known better than to think it would end differently. "I'm not moving, Walker. I'm sorry. Everything and everyone I love is here."

"I know that." He smiled. "Once I finally realized that, I knew what I had to do."

"What are you talking about?"

"I can't tell you yet. You're going to have to trust me." He caught her chin with his palm and traced the outline of her bottom lip. She wanted to lean into his touch, to kiss that warm spot on his hand, to trust him, but her mind kept telling her to be cautious, to avoid the inevitable heartbreak.

He closed the gap between them and pressed a kiss to her lips. A soft, slow, sweet kiss that tasted like sunshine on a warm spring day. "I opted for another road, Lindsay. And I hope you'll do the same."

"Another road? Walker, you're not making any sense."

He straightened. "Meet me tomorrow morning and you'll see what I'm talking about. I promise, it will be worth your time." He gave her one more kiss, then got to his feet and exited the park, leaving her with cold cocoa and a tough choice.

Chapter Thirteen

Walker had never been this nervous in his life. He'd negotiated multimillion-dollar deals, met with heads of state, jumped out of a perfectly good airplane once, but never had he been as nervous as he was on this bright October Sunday morning.

He had everything he needed, finally. It had been down to the wire, and he'd had to call in more than a few favors, but everything was done and in place. He could only pray that the decision he'd made would be met with the reaction he hoped.

He stood at the intersection of Commercial Street and South Buckskin Road, ticking off the minutes. It seemed to take forever for the hands on his watch to move.

Right at nine, Lindsay pulled up to the curb, parked her car and got out. She cupped a hand over her eyes to block the sun and gave him a quizzical look. "Why did you have me meet you at an empty lot? On a Sunday morning, at that?"

"Because it won't be empty for long. And I wanted you to see it before everything starts."

She climbed up the small grassy hill and stood before him. She had on her cowboy boots again, along with a pair of hip-hugging jeans, a pale blue V-neck shirt and a black leather jacket. She looked sexy and comfortable all at the same time, and all he wanted to do was take her home and explore every inch of her. "What everything?"

"My new corporate headquarters. We're building it from the ground up, because I couldn't find a suitable existing space in Rust Creek Falls." As he said the words, excitement filled him. It had been a long time since Walker had had a business venture that had him raring to start the day. And this one, with this incredible view, and the incredible woman before him, was the best decision he'd ever made. He was glad he'd gotten the support of the rest of the board before he made the move, because it would prevent his father from exerting control over Walker any longer. "It's not going to be some shiny, modern metal building. I'm thinking of giving it a lodge feeling, like the Maverick Manor, so it fits right in with everything else in this town. I should be starting on it next week."

"Next week?" She shook her head, and confusion filled her features again. "Wait, did you just say your *new* corporate headquarters?"

"I've decided to relocate. To right here." He pointed at the ground. "At least during my work hours. After hours, I'll be living in a house in town. A rental, for now, to give us enough time to find what we really want."

She blinked and shook her head again. "I'm confused, Walker. Why are you moving here? And renting a house here?"

"Because I don't want to leave." He took her hands in his, holding them tight. Her fingers were cold, her face wary. He couldn't blame her. He'd been distant all week, afraid to make promises he wasn't sure he could keep. But now, with everything moving forward, Walker was ready to tell Lindsay everything. "I want to stay here, right in Rust Creek Falls, with you."

She broke away from him. "Stay here? What are you doing?"

"Changing my life for the better." He tamped down his disappointment that she hadn't been overjoyed by his news. He'd thought she would be happy he was moving here, happy that he wanted to be with her.

"You don't want to live in this small town, Walker. You've told me yourself how much you love Tulsa. That you couldn't wait to get back to the city. You'll get tired of this place in a few months, and then you'll leave. And this will go back to being an empty lot."

She waved off his attempt to reach for her hand.

"Just quit—" She stopped and took in a breath, then let it out with a shudder. "Quit making me believe in things that are never going to happen."

She turned away and headed back to her car. Walker jogged down the hill and stopped in front of her. "Damn, you are a stubborn woman. What's it going to take for you to believe that I'm serious?"

"You know what I want?" She threw up her hands. "Proof. Something other than words. I've had the words before, and in the end, they weren't true. I want to know you're serious."

He chuckled. "I figured you'd say that." He reached into his back pocket and pulled out a sheaf of papers. "So here, counselor, are your exhibits, proving my case. The deed to this very plot of land. A letter from the building department, approving our architectural rendering. A lease for a rental down the street—"

"How did you accomplish all this so quickly?"

"Well, I paid some of my people very well to work extra hours, but most of the credit goes to the folks in Rust Creek Falls. Everybody knows everybody else in a place this small, and those connections can make the impossible happen." He took a step closer. "Especially when I made it clear that I want to make a long-term investment in this town. One that could benefit everyone here."

She glanced over what he had given her. "You're really doing this, aren't you?"

"That's what I've been trying to tell you."

She looked at the papers again, then at him. Her eyes widened. "You're...you're staying?"

He nodded. "There's more, Lindsay. For this one, I'm going to need a lawyer. A good lawyer, who understands this town and these people and will make sure I do this right." He reached into the opposite pocket and pulled out a handwritten list and handed it to her. "Will you set this up for me?"

She scanned the paper, the notes he'd made this morning, and her brows knitted in concentration. When she lifted her gaze to his again, surprise colored the blue depths. "You're setting up a foundation...and The Just Us Kids Pediatric Pulmonary Center? Why?"

"Because I don't want what happened to the Marshalls to happen to anyone else. Those medical bills, even with insurance, were so expensive, they could have lost their house and everything they had worked for. It could have happened to so many others, too. I thought I'd set up a foundation for the residents of Rust Creek Falls so that no one ever has to worry if they get sick. There's going to be a resource available to them to pay those bills. And a center to take their children to if they need specialized medical care. It's something this whole area needed, not just the town." Even after all he'd done for the families and for the Marshalls, Walker had felt as if he'd left something undone, that he could have done more. "I'm hoping this is a way to give back to the town that will keep on giving for years and years to come."

She softened and tears filled her eyes. "Why would you do something like that?"

He whisked away a tear with his thumb and smiled down at her. "Because you taught me to love this town as much as you do. I want to stay here, Lindsay, and build a life with you. I love you."

She opened her mouth. Closed it again. "You... love me?"

He nodded, and his heart filled with hope and a million other emotions he couldn't name. "I think I have from the minute I watched you argue in court. You were so passionate—about the case, about the people you represented, about the life you have here. And I wanted to be a part of that, with you. But most of all, I wanted to find a home. And I did, here."

"In Rust Creek Falls?"

"No." He took her in his arms. She nestled perfectly

against his chest, fitting into that space like a missing piece. Walker smiled down at her. "Right here. With you. When I see you, I feel like I've come home, and when I hold you, it's like I've found exactly the right place to be."

She pressed her head to his chest, listening to his heartbeat. He held her for a long time, while the world went on, cars passing on their way to church, families going to a big Sunday breakfast.

"I never wanted to fall in love with you," she said. "You were everything I told myself to avoid. Because I didn't want to get hurt again."

"I won't hurt you, Lindsay." He pressed a kiss to the top of her head and inhaled the floral notes of her perfume. "I spent too many years burying myself in my work because I thought what I wanted most didn't exist, and I was afraid to try and find out if it did. Then I came here, and you challenged me to step outside the comfort of my office and to really live. And love." He tipped her chin until she was looking at him. "You changed my life, Lindsay. And now I want to change yours."

He stepped back, then dropped to one knee on the grassy hill. He fished in his pocket for a red velvet box and flipped back the lid. "This was my grandmother's ring. My grandfather said that if I ever found a woman who made me want to be a better man, then I should give it to her. You have made me want to be a better person, a better business owner and most of all a better man. To give more and expect less and to leave the space around me changed for the good."

"I did all that? But...how?"

"By doing it yourself." He held the ring out to her. "So, will you marry me, Lindsay Dalton?"

She hesitated for a long moment, her fingers poised over his hand. Then she sighed and shook her head. "I can't."

The hope he'd held on to for so many days plummeted like a stone. He withdrew the box and thumbed the lid closed. "I'm sorry. I thought—"

She put a hand on his shoulder. "I can't until I show you something. Wait here." She turned and went back to her car, pulled out something big and square, then came back up the hill to him. "Considering you're renting a house here, I think this might be an appropriate housewarming gift."

He unwrapped the paper covering and revealed the painting he had tried to buy last night at the harvest festival. The Dalton ranch, nestled among the mountains and the river. "How did you get this? Vanessa said she would only sell it to a member of the Dalton family."

She shrugged. "We took a vote."

Now it was his turn to give her a confused look. "You took a vote?"

She nodded. "Me and my brothers and sister, and even my parents. Everyone heard about what you did for the kids that got sick at the day care and how you brought a ton of business to Maverick Manor. We decided that someone like that should be an honorary member of the Dalton clan, so we chipped in and bought the painting from Vanessa."

"Thank you." As much as he loved the painting, he realized that seeing it now meant seeing the memories of Lindsay and knowing she wasn't going to be his wife. Could he really look at this image every day and know that she wasn't part of the picture? "Honorary member, huh?"

She nodded. "It's a temporary status."

"How temporary?"

"However long it takes to plan a wedding." A wide smile broke across her face. "You have made a successful argument, Mr. Jones, and provided ample evidence to demonstrate your commitment to this town and to me. And I'm ruling—"

He wagged a finger in front of her. "You're not a judge."

"Might I remind you, this is an empty lot and not a court of law?" She parked her fists on her hips and gave him a stubborn smile. "So the regular rules don't apply."

"Ah, yes, indeed." He made a sweeping gesture. "Proceed, Your Honor."

"I'm ruling that you and I, given that you love me and I love you—" hearing those words made Walker's heart leap "—now enter into a binding lifetime contract. Of marriage."

He laughed. "That's one contract I'm going to sign unread."

She cocked her head to one side. "I don't know if you should. Not reading it first is a big risk."

"One I'm willing to take." He propped the painting against his leg, then took her hand again. "The question is whether you are."

"I took that risk the minute I met you, Walker Jones." She rose on her toes and kissed him. "And I realized I never want to be on the opposing side of you again."

He slid the ring onto her finger and drew her into his arms. "That's one thing that we can agree on."

She looked up at him. "So, about this rental house..."

"It's temporary, just until we find something for the two of us."

"Until then," she said, a devilish twinkle in her eyes, "I think we should go break it in. All part of the housewarming, of course."

He leaned down and kissed her, a long, deep, hot kiss that promised much more to come later. Then he drew back and tucked a stray tendril behind her ear. "Just having you there warms everything, Lindsay."

She smiled up at him. "Welcome home, Walker."

They were the words he had waited all his life to hear. His throat was thick, his heart full, and he couldn't find anything else to say. So he gathered the woman he loved into his arms and held her tight while they stood together on a grassy patch of land that was no longer empty, because now it was filled with hopes and dreams. Home, he thought, had been here all along.

* * * * *

Look for the next installment in the
Special Edition continuity

MONTANA MAVERICKS: THE BABY BONANZA

*Bella Stockton is completely surrounded by little
ones at her job at the day care center...but she can't
have a baby of her own. Could trust fund
cowboy Hudson Jones be the ideal man to heal
her broken heart?*

Don't miss

THE MAVERICK'S HOLIDAY SURPRISE

by

USA TODAY *Bestselling Author Karen Rose Smith*

*On sale November 2016
wherever Harlequin books and ebooks are sold.*

*Single mom Andrea Montgomery only agreed
to look in on injured sheriff Marshall Bailey
as a favor to his sister, but when these lonely
hearts are snowed in together, there's no
telling what Christmas wishes might come true.*

Turn the page for a sneak peek of
SNOWFALL ON HAVEN POINT
by New York Times *bestselling author*
RaeAnne Thayne,
available October 2016
wherever Harlequin books and ebooks are sold!

CHAPTER ONE

SHE REALLY NEEDED to learn how to say no once in a while.

Andrea Montgomery stood on the doorstep of the small, charming stone house just down the street from hers on Riverbend Road, her arms loaded with a tray of food that was cooling by the minute in the icy December wind blowing off the Hell's Fury River.

Her hands on the tray felt clammy and the flock of butterflies that seemed to have taken up permanent residence in her stomach jumped around maniacally. She didn't want to be here. Marshall Bailey, the man on the other side of that door, made her nervous under the best of circumstances.

This moment definitely did not fall into that category.

How could she turn down any request from Wynona Bailey, though? She owed Wynona whatever she wanted. The woman had taken a bullet for her, after all. If Wyn wanted her to march up and down the main drag in Haven Point wearing a tutu and combat boots, she would rush right out and try to find the perfect ensemble.

She would almost prefer that to Wyn's actual request but her friend had sounded desperate when she called earlier that day from Boise, where she was in graduate school to become a social worker.

"It's only for a week or so, until I can wrap things up here with my practicum and Mom and Uncle Mike make it back from their honeymoon," Wyn had said.

"It's not a problem at all," she had assured her. Apparently she was better at telling fibs than she thought because Wynona didn't even question her.

"Trust my brother to break his leg the one week that his mother and both of his sisters are completely unavailable to help him. I think he did it on purpose."

"Didn't you tell me he was struck by a hit-and-run driver?"

"Yes, but the timing couldn't be worse, with Katrina out of the country and Mom and Uncle Mike on their cruise until the end of the week. Marshall assures me he doesn't need help, but the man has a compound fracture, for crying out loud. He's not supposed to be weight-bearing at all. I would feel better the first few days he's home from the hospital if I knew that someone who lived close by could keep an eye on him."

Andie didn't want to be that someone. But how could she say no to Wynona?

It was a good thing her friend had been a police officer until recently. If Wynona had wanted a partner in crime, *Thelma & Louise* style, Andie wasn't sure she could have said no.

"Aren't you going to ring the doorbell, Mama?" Chloe asked, eyes apprehensive and her voice wavering a little. Her daughter was picking up her own nerves, Andie knew, with that weird radar kids had, but she had also become much more timid and anxious since the terrifying incident that summer when Wyn and Cade Emmett had rescued them all.

"I can do it," her four-year-old son, Will, offered. "My feet are *freezing* out here."

Her heart filled with love for both of her funny, sweet, wonderful children. Will was the spitting image of Jason while Chloe had his mouth and his eyes.

This would be their third Christmas without him and she had to hope she could make it much better than the previous two.

She repositioned the tray and forced herself to focus on the matter at hand. "Sorry, I was thinking of something else."

She couldn't very well tell her children that she hadn't knocked yet because she was too busy thinking about how much she didn't want to be here.

"I told you that Sheriff Bailey has a broken leg and can't get around very well. He probably can't make it to the door easily and I don't want to make him get up. He should be expecting us. Wynona said she was calling him."

She transferred the tray to one arm just long enough to knock a couple of times loudly and twist the doorknob, which gave way easily. The door was blessedly unlocked.

"Sheriff Bailey? Hello? It's Andrea Montgomery."

"And Will and Chloe Montgomery," her son called helpfully, and Andie had to smile, despite the nerves jangling through her.

An instant later, she heard a crash, a thud and a muffled groan.

"Sheriff Bailey?"

"Not really...a good time."

She couldn't miss the pain in the voice of Wynona's older brother. It made her realize how ridiculous she was being. The man had been through a terrible ordeal in the last twenty-four hours and all she could think about was how much he intimidated her.

Nice, Andie. Feeling small and ashamed, she set the tray down on the nearest flat surface, a small table in the foyer still decorated in Wyn's quirky, fun style even though her brother had been living in the home since late August.

"Kids, wait right here for a moment," she said.

Chloe immediately planted herself on the floor by the door, her features taking on the fearful look she had worn too frequently since Rob Warren burst back into their lives so violently. Will, on the other hand, looked bored already. How had her children's roles reversed so abruptly? Chloe used to be the brave one, charging enthusiastically past any challenge, while Will had been the more tentative child.

"Do you need help?" Chloe asked tentatively.

"No. Stay here. I'll be right back."

She was sure the sound had come from the room where Wyn had spent most of her time when she lived here, a space that served as den, family room and TV viewing room in one. Her gaze immediately went to Marshall Bailey, trying to heft himself back up to the sofa from the floor.

"Oh no!" she exclaimed. "What happened?"

"What do you think happened?" he growled. "You knocked on the door, so I tried to get up to answer and the damn crutches slipped out from under me."

"I'm so sorry. I only knocked to give you a little

warning before we barged in. I didn't mean for you to get up."

He glowered. "Then you shouldn't have come over and knocked on the door."

She hated any conversation that came across as a confrontation. They always made her want to hide away in her room like she was a teenager again in her grandfather's house. It was completely immature of her, she knew. Grown-ups couldn't always walk away.

"Wyn asked me to check on you. Didn't she tell you?"

"I haven't talked to her since yesterday. My phone ran out of juice and I haven't had a chance to charge it."

By now, the county sheriff had pulled himself back onto the sofa and was trying to position pillows for his leg that sported a black orthopedic boot from his toes to just below his knee. His features contorted as he tried to reach the pillows but he quickly smoothed them out again. The man was obviously in pain and doing his best to conceal it.

She couldn't leave him to suffer, no matter how nervous his gruff demeanor made her.

She hurried forward and pulled the second pillow into place. "Is that how you wanted it?" she asked.

"For now."

She had a sudden memory of seeing the sheriff the night Rob Warren had broken into her home, assaulted her, held her at gunpoint and ended up in a shoot-out with the Haven Point police chief, Cade Emmett. He had burst into her home after the situation had been largely defused, to find Cade on the ground trying to revive a bleeding Wynona.

The stark fear on Marshall's face had haunted her, knowing that she might have unwittingly contributed to him losing another sibling after he had already lost his father and a younger brother in the line of duty.

Now Marshall's features were a shade or two paler and his eyes had the glassy, distant look of someone in a great deal of pain.

"How long have you been out of the hospital?"

He shrugged. "A couple hours. Give or take."

"And you're here by yourself?" she exclaimed. "I thought you were supposed to be home earlier this morning and someone was going to stay with you for the first few hours. Wynona told me that was the plan."

"One of my deputies drove me home from the hospital but I told him Chief Emmett would probably keep an eye on me."

The police chief lived across the street from Andie and just down the street from Marshall, which boded well for crime prevention in the neighborhood. Having the sheriff *and* the police chief on the same street should be any sane burglar's worst nightmare—especially *this* particular sheriff and police chief.

"And has he been by?"

"Uh, no. I didn't ask him to." Marshall's eyes looked unnaturally blue in his pain-tight features. "Did my sister send you to babysit me?"

"Babysit, no. She only asked me to periodically check on you. I also brought dinner for the next few nights."

"Also unnecessary. If I get hungry, I'll call Serrano's for a pizza later."

She gave him a bland look. "Would a pizza delivery driver know to come pick you up off the floor?"

"You didn't pick me up," he muttered. "You just moved a few pillows around."

He must find this completely intolerable, being dependent on others for the smallest thing. In her limited experience, most men made difficult patients. Tough, take-charge guys like Marshall Bailey probably hated every minute of it.

Sympathy and compassion had begun to replace some of her nervousness. She would probably never truly like the man—he was so big, so masculine, a cop through and through—but she could certainly empathize with what he was going through. For now, he was a victim and she certainly knew what that felt like.

"I brought dinner, so you might as well eat it," she said. "You can order pizza tomorrow if you want. It's not much, just beef stew and homemade rolls, with caramel apple pie for dessert."

"Not much?" he said, eyebrow raised. A low rumble sounded in the room just then and it took her a moment to realize it was coming from his stomach.

"You don't have to eat it, but if you'd like some, I can bring it in here."

He opened his mouth but before he could answer, she heard a voice from the doorway.

"What happened to you?" Will asked, gazing at Marshall's assorted scrapes, bruises and bandages with wide-eyed fascination.

"Will, I thought I told you to wait for me by the door."

"I know, but you were taking *forever*." He walked

into the room a little farther, not at all intimidated by the battered, dangerous-looking man it contained. "Hi. My name is Will. What's yours?"

The sheriff gazed at her son. If anything, his features became even more remote, but he might have simply been in pain.

"This is Sheriff Bailey," Andie said, when Marshall didn't answer for a beat too long. "He's Wynona's brother."

Will beamed at him as if Marshall was his new best friend. "Wynona is nice and she has a nice dog whose name is Young Pete, only Wynona said he's not young anymore."

"Yeah, I know Young Pete," Marshall said after another pause. "He's been in our family for a long time. He was our dad's dog first."

Andie gave him a careful look. From Wyn, she knew their father had been shot in the line of duty several years earlier and had suffered a severe brain injury that left him physically and cognitively impaired. John Bailey had died the previous winter from pneumonia, after spending his last years at a Shelter Springs care center.

Though she had never met the man, her heart ached to think of all the Baileys had suffered.

"Why is his name Young Pete?" Will asked. "I think that's silly. He should be just Pete."

"Couldn't agree more, but you'll have to take that up with my sister."

Will accepted that with equanimity. He took another step closer and scrutinized the sheriff. "How did you get so hurt? Were you in a fight with some bad guys? Did you shoot them? A bad guy came to our house once and Chief Emmett shot him."

Andie stepped in quickly. She was never sure how much Will understood about what happened that summer. "Will, I need your help fixing a tray with dinner for the sheriff."

"I want to hear about the bad guys, though."

"There were no bad guys. I was hit by a car," Marshall said abruptly.

"You're big! Don't you know you're supposed to look both ways and hold someone's hand?"

Marshall Bailey's expression barely twitched. "I guess nobody happened to be around at the time."

Torn between amusement and mortification, Andie grabbed her son's hand. "Come on, Will," she said, her tone insistent. "I need your help."

Her put-upon son sighed. "Okay."

He let her hold his hand as they went back to the entry, where Chloe still sat on the floor, watching the hallway with anxious eyes.

"I told Will not to go in when you told us to wait here but he wouldn't listen to me," Chloe said fretfully.

"You should see the police guy," Will said with relish. "He has blood on him and everything."

Andie hadn't seen any blood but maybe Will was more observant than she. Or maybe he had just become good at trying to get a rise out of his sister.

"Ew. Gross," Chloe exclaimed, looking at the doorway with an expression that contained equal parts revulsion and fascination.

"He is Wyn's brother and knows Young Pete, too," Will informed her.

Easily distracted, as most six-year-old girls could

be, Chloe sighed. "I miss Young Pete. I wonder if he and Sadie will be friends?"

"Why wouldn't they be?" Will asked.

"Okay, kids, we can talk about Sadie and Young Pete another time. Right now, we need to get dinner for Wynona's brother."

"I need to use the bathroom," Will informed her. He had that urgent look he sometimes wore when he had pushed things past the limit.

"There's a bathroom just down the hall, second door down. See?"

"Okay."

He raced for it—she hoped in time.

"We'll be in the kitchen," she told him, then carried the food to the bright and spacious room with its stainless appliances and white cabinets.

"See if you can find a small plate for the pie while I dish up the stew," she instructed Chloe.

"Okay," her daughter said.

The nervous note in her voice broke Andie's heart, especially when she thought of the bold child who used to run out to confront the world.

"Do I have to carry it out there?" Chloe asked.

"Not if you don't want to, honey. You can wait right here in the kitchen or in the entryway, if you want."

While Chloe perched on one of the kitchen stools and watched, Andie prepared a tray for him, trying to make it as tempting as possible. She had a feeling his appetite wouldn't be back to normal for a few days because of the pain and the aftereffects of anesthesia but at least the fault wouldn't lie in her presentation.

It didn't take long, but it still gave her time to make note of the few changes in the kitchen. In the few months Wynona had been gone, Marshall Bailey had left his mark. The kitchen was clean but not sparkling, and where Wyn had kept a cheery bowl of fruit on the counter, a pair of handcuffs and a stack of mail cluttered the space. Young Pete's food and water bowls were presumably in Boise with Young Pete.

As she looked at the space on the floor where they usually rested, she suddenly remembered dogs weren't the only creatures who needed beverages.

"I forgot to fill Sheriff Bailey's water bottle," she said to Chloe. "Could you do that for me?"

Chloe hopped down from her stool and picked up the water bottle. With her bottom lip pressed firmly between her teeth, she filled the water bottle with ice and water from the refrigerator before screwing the lid back on and held it out for Andie.

"Thanks, honey. Oh, the tray's pretty full and I don't have a free hand. I guess I'll have to make another trip for it."

As she had hoped, Chloe glanced at the tray and then at the doorway with trepidation on her features that eventually shifted to resolve.

"I guess I can maybe carry it for you," she whispered.

Andie smiled and rubbed a hand over her hair, heart bursting with pride at this brave little girl. "Thank you, Chloe. You're always such a big help to me."

Chloe mustered a smile, though it didn't stick. "You'll be right there?"

"The whole time. Where do you suppose that brother of yours is?"

She suspected the answer, even before she and

Chloe walked back to the den and she heard Will chattering.

"And I want a new Lego set and a sled and some real walkie-talkies like my friend Ty has. He has his own pony and I want one of those, too, only my mama says I can't have one because we don't have a place for him to run. Ty lives on a ranch and we only have a little backyard and we don't have a barn or any hay for him to eat. That's what horses eat—did you know that?"

Rats. Had she actually been stupid enough to fall for that "I have to go to the bathroom" gag? She should have known better. Will had probably raced right back in here the moment her back was turned.

"I did know that. And oats and barley, too," Sheriff Bailey said. His voice, several octaves below Will's, rippled down her spine. Did he sound annoyed? She couldn't tell. Mostly, his voice sounded remote.

"We have oatmeal at our house and my mom puts barley in soup sometimes, so why couldn't we have a pony?"

She should probably rescue the man. He just had one leg broken by a hit-and-run driver. He didn't need the other one talked off by an almost-five-year-old. She moved into the room just in time to catch the tail end of the discussion.

"A pony is a pretty big responsibility," Marshall said.

"So is a dog and a cat and we have one of each, a dog named Sadie and a cat named Mrs. Finnegan," Will pointed out.

"But a pony is a lot more work than a dog *or* a cat. Anyway, how would one fit on Santa's sleigh?"

Judging by his peal of laughter, Will apparently thought that was hilarious.

"He couldn't! You're silly."

She had to wonder if anyone had ever called the serious sheriff *silly* before. She winced and carried the tray inside the room, judging it was past time to step in.

"Here you go. Dinner. Again, don't get your hopes up. I'm an adequate cook but that's about it."

She set the food down on the end table next to the sofa and found a folded wooden TV tray she didn't remember from her frequent visits to the house when Wynona lived here. She set up the TV tray and transferred the food to it, then gestured for Chloe to bring the water bottle. Her daughter hurried over without meeting his gaze, set the bottle on the tray, then rushed back to the safety of the kitchen as soon as she could.

Marshall looked at the tray, then at her, leaving her feeling as if *she* were the silly one.

"Thanks. It looks good. I appreciate your kindness," he said stiffly, as if the words were dragged out of him.

He had to know any kindness on her part was out of obligation toward Wynona. The thought made her feel rather guilty. He was her neighbor and she should be more enthusiastic about helping him, whether he made her nervous or not.

"Where is your cell phone?" she asked. "You need some way to contact the outside world."

"Why?"

She frowned. "Because people are concerned about you! You just got out of the hospital a few hours ago. You need pain medicine at regular intervals and you're

probably supposed to have ice on that leg or something."

"I'm fine, as long as I can get to the bathroom and
the kitchen and I have the remote close at hand."

Such a typical man. She huffed out a breath. "At
least think of the people who care about you. Wyn
is out of her head with worry, especially since your
mother and Katrina aren't in town."

"Why do you think I didn't charge my phone?"
he muttered.

She crossed her arms across her chest. She didn't
like confrontation or big, dangerous men any more
than her daughter did, but Wynona had asked her to
watch out for him and she took the charge seriously.

"You're being obstinate. What if you trip over your
crutches and hit your head, only this time somebody
isn't at the door to make sure you can get up again?"

"That's not going to happen."

"You don't know that. Where is your phone, Sheriff?"

He glowered at her but seemed to accept the inevitable. "Fine," he said with a sigh. "It should be in
the pocket of my jacket, which is in the bag they sent
home with me from the hospital. I think my deputy
said he left it in the bedroom. First door on the left."

The deputy should have made sure his boss had
some way to contact the outside world, but she had
a feeling it was probably a big enough chore getting
Sheriff Bailey home from the hospital without him
trying to drive himself and she decided to give the
poor guy some slack.

"I'm going to assume the charger is in there, too."

"Yeah. By the bed."

She walked down the hall to the room that had once been Wyn's bedroom. The bedroom still held traces of Wynona in the solid Mission furniture set but Sheriff Bailey had stamped his own personality on it in the last three months. A Stetson hung on one of the bedposts, and instead of mounds of pillows and the beautiful log cabin quilt Wyn's aunts had made her, a no-frills but soft-looking navy duvet covered the bed, made neatly as he had probably left it the morning before. A pile of books waited on the bedside table and a pair of battered cowboy boots stood toe-out next to the closet.

The room smelled masculine and entirely too sexy for her peace of mind, of sage-covered mountains with an undertone of leather and spice.

Except for that brief moment when she had helped him back to the sofa, she had never been close enough to Marshall to see if that scent clung to his skin. The idea made her shiver a little before she managed to rein in the wholly inappropriate reaction.

She found the plastic hospital bag on the wide armchair near the windows, overlooking the snow-covered pines along the river. Feeling strangely guilty at invading the man's privacy, she opened it. At the top of the pile that appeared to contain mostly clothing, she found another large clear bag with a pair of ripped jeans inside covered in a dried dark substance she realized was blood.

Marshall Bailey's blood.

The stark reminder of his close call sent a tremor through her. He could have been killed if that hit-and-run driver had struck him at a slightly higher rate of speed. The Baileys likely wouldn't have recovered, especially since Wyn's twin brother, Wyatt, had been struck and killed by an out-of-control vehicle while helping a stranded motorist during a winter storm.

The jeans weren't ruined beyond repair. Maybe she could spray stain remover on them and try to mend the rips and tears.

Further searching through the bag finally unearthed the telephone. She found the charger next to the bed and carried the phone, charger and bag containing the Levi's back to the sheriff.

While she was gone from the room, he had pulled the tray close and was working on the dinner roll in a desultory way.

She plugged the charger into the same outlet as the lamp next to the sofa and inserted the other end into his phone. "Here you are. I'll let you turn it on. Now you'll have no excuse not to talk to your family when they call."

"Thanks. I guess."

Andie held out the bag containing the jeans. "Do you mind if I take these? I'd like to see if I can get the stains out and do a little repair work."

"It's not worth the effort. I don't even know why they sent them home. The paramedics had to cut them away to get to my leg."

"You never know. I might be able to fix them."

He shrugged, his eyes wearing that distant look again. He was in pain, she realized, and trying very hard not to show it.

"If you power on your phone and unlock it, I can put my cell number in there so you can reach me in an emergency."

"I won't—" he started to say but the sentence ended with a sigh as he reached for the phone.

As soon as he turned it on, the phone gave a cacophony of beeps, alerting him to missed texts and messages, but he paid them no attention.

"What's your number?"

She gave it to him and in turn entered his into her own phone.

"Please don't be stubborn. If you need help, call me. I'm just a few houses away and can be here in under two minutes—and that's even if I have to take time to put on boots and a winter coat."

He likely wouldn't call and both of them knew it.

"Are we almost done?" Will asked from the doorway, clearly tired of having only his sister to talk to in the other room.

"In a moment," she said, then turned back to Marshall. "Do you know Herm and Louise Jacobs, next door?"

Oddly, he gaped at her for a long, drawn-out moment. "Why do you ask?" His voice was tight with suspicion.

"If I'm not around and you need help for some reason, they or their grandson Christopher can be here even faster. I'll put their number in your phone, too, just in case."

"I doubt I'll need it, but...thanks."

"Christopher has a skateboard, a big one," Will offered gleefully. "He rides it without even a helmet!"

Her son had a bad case of hero worship when it came to the Jacobses' troubled grandson, who had come to live with Herm and Louise shortly after Andie and her children arrived in Haven Point. It worried her a little to see how fascinated Will was with the clearly rebellious teenager, but so far Christopher had been patient and even kind to her son.

"That's not very safe, is it?" the sheriff said gruffly. "You should always wear a helmet when you're riding a bike or skateboard to protect your head."

"I don't even *have* a skateboard," Will said.

"If you get one," Marshall answered. This time she couldn't miss the clear strain in his voice. The man was at the end of his endurance and probably wanted nothing more than to be alone with his pain.

"We really do need to leave," Andie said quickly. "Is there anything else I can do to help you before we leave?"

He shook his head, then winced a little as if the motion hurt. "You've done more than enough already."

"Try to get some rest, if you can. I'll check in with you tomorrow and also bring something for your lunch."

He didn't exactly look overjoyed at the prospect. "I don't suppose I can say anything to persuade you otherwise, can I?"

"You're a wise man, Sheriff Bailey."

Will giggled. "Where's your gold and Frankenstein?"

Marshall blinked, obviously as baffled as she was, which only made Will giggle more.

"Like in the Baby Jesus story, you know. The wise men brought the gold, Frankenstein and mirth."

She did her best to hide a smile. This year Will had become fascinated with the small carved Nativity set she bought at a thrift store the first year she moved out of her grandfather's cheerless house.

"Oh. Frankincense and myrrh. They were perfumes and oils, I think. When I said Sheriff Bailey was a wise man, I just meant he was smart."

She was a little biased, yes, but she couldn't believe even the most hardened of hearts wouldn't find her son adorable. The sheriff only studied them both with that dour expression.

He was in pain, she reminded herself. If she were in his position, she wouldn't find a four-year-old's chatter amusing, either.

"We'll see you tomorrow," she said again. "Call me, even if it's the middle of the night."

"I will," he said, which she knew was a blatant fib. He would never call her.

She had done all she could, short of moving into his house—kids, pets and all.

She gathered the children part of that equation and ushered them out of the house. Darkness came early this close to the winter solstice but the Jacobs family's Christmas lights next door gleamed through the snow.

In the short time she'd been inside his house, Andie had forgotten most of her nervousness around Marshall. Perhaps it was his injury that made him feel a little less threatening to her—though she had a feeling that even if he'd suffered *two* broken legs in that accident, the sheriff of Lake Haven County would never be anything less than dangerous.

COMING NEXT MONTH FROM

H HARLEQUIN®

SPECIAL EDITION

Available October 18, 2016

#2509 A CHILD UNDER HIS TREE
Return to the Double C • by Allison Leigh
Kelly Rasmussen and Caleb Buchanan were high school sweethearts until life
got in the way. Now they're both back in Weaver and want a second chance, but
everything is made more complicated by the five-year-old little boy with his secret
father's eyes.

#2510 THE MAVERICK'S HOLIDAY SURPRISE
Montana Mavericks: The Baby Bonanza • by Karen Rose Smith
Trust-fund cowboy Hudson Jones wants Bella Stockton, but day-care babies and a
secret stand in their way. Can Hudson help Bella overcome her intimacy fears—and
can Bella convince the roaming cowboy that home for the holidays is the best place
to be?

#2511 THE RANCHER'S EXPECTANT CHRISTMAS
Wed in the West • by Karen Templeton
When jilted—and hugely pregnant—Deanna Blake returns to Whispering Pines,
New Mexico, for her father's funeral, single dad Josh Talbot sees everything he
wants in a partner in the grown-up version of his old friend. But how can this
uncomplicated country boy heal the city girl's broken heart?

#2512 CALLIE'S CHRISTMAS WISH
Three Coins in the Fountain • by Merline Lovelace
Callie Langston is *not* boring! And to prove it, she's going to Rome to work as a
counselor to female refugees over Christmas. Security expert Joe Russo learned
the hard way how cruel the world can be when his fiancé was murdered, and he
plans on making sure Callie is protected—always. Even if that means he has to
follow her halfway around the globe. But can Callie's thirst for adventure and Joe's
protective instincts coexist long enough for her Christmas wish to come true?

#2513 THANKFUL FOR YOU
The Brands of Montana • by Joanna Sims
Dallas Dalton wants to mess up city-boy lawyer Nick Brand's perfectly controlled
exterior from the moment they meet. Nick can't explain why he's drawn to the wild-
child cowgirl, he just knows he is. But they come from completely different worlds,
and it might just take a Thanksgiving miracle to prove to them they have more in
common than they think.

#2514 THE COWBOY'S BIG FAMILY TREE
Hurley's Homestyle Kitchen • by Meg Maxwell
Christmas is coming and rancher Logan Grainger is struggling with the news that
another man is his biological father. He recently became guardian to his orphaned
nephews and learned that his new nine-year-old stepsister is being fostered by his
old flame Clementine Hurley. She wants them to be a family, but can Logan move
past the lies to bring them all together under a Christmas tree?

YOU CAN FIND MORE INFORMATION ON UPCOMING HARLEQUIN® TITLES,
FREE EXCERPTS AND MORE AT WWW.HARLEQUIN.COM.

HSECNM1016

"Why do you care, Caleb?"

He was silent for so long she wasn't sure he was going to answer. And since he wasn't, she pushed away from the brick. "I need to get back to Tyler."

"I've always cared."

His words washed over her. Instead of feeling like a balmy wave, though, it felt like being rolled against abrasive sand. "Right." She stepped around him.

"Dammit." His hand shot out and he grabbed her arm.

She tried to shaking him off. "Let go."

"You asked and I'm telling you. So now you're going to walk away?" He let her go. "I swear, you're as stubborn as your mother."

She flinched.

He swore again. Thrust his fingers through his dark hair. "I didn't mean that."

Why not? She adored her son. Didn't regret his existence for one single second. In that, she was very different from her mother. But that didn't mean she wasn't Georgette Rasmussen's daughter with all the rest that that implied.

"I have to go." She tried stepping around his big body again.

"I'm sorry that I hurt you. I was always sorry, Kelly. Always."

She looked up at him. "But you did it anyway."

"And you're going to hate me forever because of it? It was nearly ten years ago!"

When he'd dumped her for another girl.

And only six years when she'd impetuously, angrily put her mouth on his and set in motion a situation she still couldn't change.

Which was worse?

His actions or hers?

Her eyes suddenly burned. Because she was pretty sure keeping the existence of his own son from him outweighed him falling in love with someone far better suited to him than simple little Kelly Rasmussen.

He made a rough sound of impatience. "If you're gonna hate me anyway—"

She barely had a chance to frown before his mouth hit hers.

Don't miss
A CHILD UNDER HIS TREE by Allison Leigh,
available November 2016 wherever
Harlequin® Special Edition books and ebooks are sold.

www.Harlequin.com

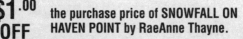

Harlequin has everything from contemporary, passionate and heartwarming to suspenseful and inspirational stories.

Whatever your mood,
we have a romance just for you!

Connect with us to find your next great read,
special offers and more.